The Yoghurt Plot

Also by Fleur Hitchcock

Shrunk!
Shrunk! Meteorites and Mayhem
The Trouble with Mummies

FLEUR HITCHCOCK

HOT
KEY
BOOKS

First published in Great Britain in 2014 by Hot Key Books
Northburgh House, 10 Northburgh Street, London EC1V 0AT

A CIP catalogue record for this book is available from the British Library.

ISBN: 978-1-4714-0324-8

1

This book is typeset in 11pt Sabon using Atomik ePublisher

Printed and bound by Clays Ltd, St Ives Plc

FSC

Hot Key Books supports the Forest Stewardship Council (FSC),
the leading international forest certification organisation, and is
committed to printing only on Greenpeace-approved FSC-certified paper.

www.hotkeybooks.com

Hot Key Books is part of the Bonnier Publishing Group
www.bonnierpublishing.com

For G.M.H. & Auntie Norah

Chapter 1

Hello.

My name is Bugg.

Jitterbug.

Don't laugh; it's not supposed to be a joke. It's a dance.

Since Monday we live at number 1, Cherry Blossom Avenue, Shabbiton.

The town has a pier (burned-out), a shopping centre (mostly closed), a car showroom (shiny), a skateboard park (really a building site), a huge sandy beach, a bank of pebbles and a nuclear power station (disused).

We have, in our house, among other things, a bedroom (that I share with Dad's paperwork), a TV (with Granddad glued to it), six skateboards (four with wheels) and a fridge, a large, cream, enamelled fridge that hums and whistles and stands in the corner of the kitchen. It has two plastic letters on it. An *A* and a *T*.

I mention the fridge, because I just tried to turn it off.

But it won't. It won't switch off. When I flick up the switch on the wall, it goes on humming and whistling, and the light inside turns on when you open the door. I've checked to see that there's only one cable, and there is. It just won't switch off.

Granddad's watching telly at full volume in his dressing gown and pyjamas. He's also eating noodles. He sucks them through a gap in his teeth, one at a time, the longest ones first, the shorter ones later.

'Have you seen Dilan?' I ask.

Granddad pauses mid-noodle and glances over to me. He shakes his head and draws the end of the noodle through the tiny gap in his lips. It makes a kissing sound as it disappears.

'Dilan?' I yell up the stairs and then, when there's no answer, clamber past the folded removal boxes until I reach his room.

There's no sign of Dilan. No sign of Dilan himself, just a crumpled school uniform on the floor, some headphones and a pair of crusty socks.

Even from up here I can hear Granddad's music. I can't actually pick out the tunes, but it's like living over an old-fashioned disco, all day and almost all night.

I look out of the window. There's a thick sea mist blowing over the town, making the house feel as if it's on its own island. I can barely see over the fence, but I know Dilan's out there on his skateboard. He says the road here's better for skateboarding than where we lived before, which was only two hundred yards away in the estate. He says living in a cul-de-sac makes it more fun. It's definitely quieter – hardly any cars – and now we've got a proper garden with an apple tree and a shed, and the house has room downstairs, so that Granddad can stay with us all the time and not be lonely any more.

And the fridge. We've got a bigger fridge.

I open the window. 'Dilan! Can you come in?'

He thumps down one end of the skateboard. 'Why?'

I look up and down the street. There isn't anyone to see, but I don't want anyone to hear me. 'Just, could you?'

Dilan lets out a sigh. 'What is it now?' he says, balancing on one pair of wheels.

I close the window and wait. I'm not going down again until Dilan comes in. I'm not going to be on my own with the fridge.

Someone opens the front door and, although I know it's Dilan, I jump.

'Bugg!' he yells up the stairs. 'This had better be good. I'm not searching under the bed again, or the cupboard, or the cellar – do it yourself.'

I jump down the stairs, my feet together, thumping in time to Granddad's TV music.

'It's the fridge,' I say.

'The fridge?' says Dilan, kicking off his shoes. 'What do you mean, the fridge? Is there something living underneath it? What is it?'

'It won't turn off,' I say. 'It's alive.'

'Why did you even try to turn it off?'

'Because it was making these horrible noises – sort of *weeeeeeeep*, and *whooooooo*, and *cccccccccccccccccc*.'

Dilan shakes his head. 'What are you on about?'

I walk through the sitting room, passing Granddad, who

is sitting on the floor by the TV. He's left the noodles on a side table, and is flicking through a pile of ballroom-dancing DVDs. I know he's watched them all a hundred times before, but Mum says it gives him comfort, so Dilan and I are learning to leave him to it.

'Where's this fridge then?' says Dilan, behind me.

I lead him into the kitchen, a room he never visits if he can help it. I'm scared of monsters, but Dilan's scared of washing up.

Actually, Dilan's scared of soap and water – I don't think he's had a shower for more than two months.

We stop in front of the fridge. 'OK,' I say, 'watch.' And I unplug the fridge.

The little red light on the front stays lit.

'That could just be a time-delay thing,' he says. 'My phone takes ages to turn off.'

'Does it really take this long? I switched it off five minutes ago.'

Dilan obviously doesn't believe me.

'What about this then?' I ask, swinging the door open. The inside light pings on, illuminating the butter dish.

Dilan raises an eyebrow.

'And listen,' I say. 'Listen to it.'

We stand in silence. Granddad's dance music shakes the thin wooden walls of the house. The fridge hums. It whistles, it burps, it sings. It's as if it knows what Granddad is listening to; it's even in tune.

Eeeeeeeeeeeee

Ooooooooooooooooh

Fsssssssssssssssssh

We listen for minutes, and the noise goes on.

Sweeeeeeeeeeeeeee

'That doesn't make sense,' says Dilan, walking around the fridge, checking for wires. 'Ah,' he says, 'it must be plugged in underneath.'

I hadn't thought of that. He checks for wires by nudging the fridge out from the wall and sliding a fish slice underneath. He scoops out a green plastic C. No wires. He arranges the letters on the fridge door.

CAT.

'See?' I say. 'It won't turn off.'

'It must be rechargeable,' he says. 'It must have a battery.'

I hadn't thought of that either and together we pull it right out so that we can look behind. But there's no room for a battery, and there's no switch, just a squashed red thing that was probably once a tomato.

We stand, staring at the back of the fridge, listening to it singing and humming, and sounding . . . human.

'I think,' says Dilan, 'that you might be right. It is alive. We have bought a house with a living fridge.' As he says it, the door springs open.

Chapter 2

I jump. I jump right out of the kitchen, into the hall.

Dilan turns and raises an eyebrow. 'It's only a fridge, Bugg.'

Mum bursts in through the door behind us, shopping bags dangling from her wrists. 'Gosh, it's foggy out there, never known one like it. Your poor granddad would call it a pea-souper.'

'Mum,' says Dilan, 'this fridge doesn't seem to need electricity to run. And the door opens – on its own.' He glares at me.

Mum wrinkles her nose. 'Really? That can't possibly be true.'

'Look, we unplugged it. The light still works.' He opens the door wide. Inside, apart from yellowed plastic, the fridge looks normal. It's almost completely empty except for a shelf of yoghurts with foil lids and the last scrap of butter smeared on the butter dish.

'How odd,' says Mum, stepping back and rustling the shopping bags. 'Well, there must be some explanation. It *was* running when we arrived, and those yoghurts were there. I haven't had the heart to throw them away.' She reaches past

12

me to pick one up. 'They haven't swelled up or anything, and I know that yoghurt keeps for ages.' She holds the yoghurt at a distance, studying the label. 'Funny – they're almost retro – like the yoghurts on the TV when I was a child.' She puts it back on the shelf. 'Sort this shopping away for me, dears. I'm just going to see your granddad.'

We empty the bags. Dilan does the cold food and I do the cupboards. The fridge hums almost tunefully. It feels like we're sharing the room with another person.

'Right,' says Dilan, looking down at all the things that won't fit.

'Take the yoghurts out,' I say. 'We don't really want them in there – do we? They must be toxic by now.'

He shuffles the contents until the yoghurts come out, and they stand on the side – a row of eight waxy cartons.

'Hmm,' says Dilan. 'These are . . .'

'Old?' I say, picking up one of the yoghurt pots. I examine it for a sell-by date. It doesn't have one. It doesn't even have ingredients on it. There's a faded yellow picture of what could be a peach; that's all.

Dilan holds another. It might be blackberry flavoured – or it might be coal dust; the picture's so bad I can't tell.

'Dare you to open it,' he says, holding it out under my nose. I look down at the top. It's a foil lid with the word YOGHURT printed across it in blue capitals. Not even the slightest hint of a flavour. It could contain anything. It could contain a monster from a distant galaxy. Admittedly, it would be a very small one.

'No,' I say.

'Scaredy-cat,' he says.

I stare at the yoghurt pot. It's too small to house anything really lethal.

Surely.

The clock on the wall ticks away the seconds. The fridge sets up a new tune. Idly, I rearrange the plastic letters on the fridge. ACT.

I turn the yoghurt upright, hold my breath and peel back the corner of the foil.

Nothing happens. It doesn't explode – nothing climbs out of the pot.

We peer inside. 'It looks exactly like ordinary yoghurt,' says Dilan. 'There was no *pft* when you took off the top; it's fine.' He looks disappointed. 'It isn't even full of alien bacteria, unless alien bacteria don't act immediately and are in fact *slow-release alien bacteria*. Like one of those plug-in air fresheners.'

I ignore Dilan and stare into the pot.

'Dare you,' he says.

'Dare you back,' I say.

'Double dare,' he says.

So I take a spoon from the drawer and dip it into the yoghurt.

A yellowy blob trembles on the bowl of the spoon.

'Double double triple dare,' he says, his eyes wide and fixed on my mouth.

'OK,' I say, and drop the yoghurt onto my tongue.

Nothing happens. Nothing – except that, not to be outdone, Dilan rips the lid from his pot. His is a mild lilac colour. He plunges the spoon deep inside and takes almost half the contents in a single mouthful.

'That –' he says. 'That's delicious – best yoghurt I've ever tasted.'

I dip the spoon deeper into my pot. I can't work out the taste. Is it peach – or pear? Or maybe apricot? I peer at the outside of the pot. The label really doesn't tell me anything. There isn't even a company name, and the picture is so indistinct it might as well be a fried egg. And then I see faint numbers on the side. A one, a nine, a seven and a four.

'1974?' I say, pointing to the pot. 'It can't be that old.'

Dilan tilts his yoghurt and examines it. He stares for a long time, long enough for me to scrape the last smears from the inside of my pot and then run my tongue around the inside, just to make sure.

'It might say 1-9-7-4 – but it can't be a sell-by date. They hadn't invented them then. We studied that in food tech. Perhaps it's some sort of inspection code. You know, like clothes have numbers on them, to say who checked them.'

I shrug. I look towards the countertop, where the other six yoghurts are.

Except they're not there. The countertop's not there either.

'Dilan,' I whisper.

'What?' he says, running his tongue around the inside of his yoghurt pot.

'Look.'

'What at?'

I gaze around at what ought to be our kitchen. 'Everything.'

Chapter 3

I grip the fridge door. It's the same fridge – it's grubbier – but definitely the same.

'Oh,' says Dilan next to me. 'What . . . ?'

I turn slowly till my back's to the fridge and look around the room. It's a kitchen. The cooker's in the same place. The sink's in the same place, but they aren't the same cooker or sink. Where the wooden countertop with flush under-cupboards should be, is a pale blue version of the same thing. Where the cottage-rose tiles covered the walls, is orange paint. The kitchen table seems to have turned from wood to plastic. The chairs have developed vinyl squashy seats and dented metal legs. The kettle has shed its plastic outside and become a bare metal pointy thing with a huge plug hanging out of the back.

Something grey boils on the cooker. The stink coming out of the pan catches in my throat: a thick mix of dishcloths and old meat.

Even the floor's gone. It was tiled; now it's blue and white squares.

'A cat,' whispers Dilan, pointing. 'We don't have a cat.'

The cat gazes at us. Lifts up a hind leg, licks its bottom and then slips out through the slightly open back door.

'C'mon,' says Dilan. 'Let's get out of here – we need fresh air.'

'Shhh,' I say. 'Listen.'

'I can't hear anything,' he says.

'Exactly,' I say. 'What's happened to Granddad?'

Leaving the yoghurt pots on the strange blue countertop, Dilan steps towards the lounge door. I'm sure it was wood, but now it seems to be wobbly glass. Through it I can see an orange carpet and some brown shapes.

He puts his hand on the handle.

'Don't,' I say.

'It's our house,' he whispers back.

I pause in the middle of the kitchen. I'd like to run, but I want to know who's in the living room. I sort of want it to be Granddad, but then again, I sort of don't.

Dilan presses down the handle. The door clicks, and there's the faintest brushing sound as it rubs across the carpet. Dilan glances back towards me before sticking his curly head through the gap. He stops with his head still visible from my side and slowly draws back, pulling the door and leaving it just short of closed.

He points towards the back door and I follow him, tiptoeing across the kitchen and out into the garden.

And there's another surprise. The elderly apple tree with our washing line attached seems to have been replaced with a much smaller one. The driveway is covered in grass, with a shiny old-fashioned car on it, and the fence is in fact a hedge.

Dilan points towards the road and we race out onto the rutted gravel track.

'Whoa,' says Dilan staring at the ground beneath his feet. 'It was tarmac ten minutes ago.'

'And that,' I say, pointing at a building site stretching away towards a distant wood, 'was houses.'

We stare. We stand and we stare, and the more we do it, and the longer I have to think about what's happening, the sicker I feel.

'It wasn't Granddad,' says Dilan eventually.

'No?' I say, unsurprised.

'No. It was a fat bloke asleep in front of the telly – watching something in black and white.'

'Oh,' I say. 'Did you recognise him?'

Dilan shakes his head. 'He was big, ugly, with sideburns, not at all like Granddad – but it wasn't just that – the whole room had changed. There was loads of random orange furniture and a really nasty carpet, and, Bugg – the weirdest thing was that the conservatory was gone.'

'Gone?' I turn back towards the house and peer through the hedge. Dilan's right. The conservatory isn't there – and not only that, judging by the buttercups sticking their heads through the grass, it hasn't been there for a while.

I sit on a tree stump that I don't remember being there. In the distance I can see the sea, the town, the pier, although the pier looks different; there seems to be more of it. In fact, the burned-out pier that's been losing bits in winter storms for my entire life seems to be complete, with flags and towers and everything. I scan the view. For the first time

18

ever, I see the digger that sits on the shingle bank move. It takes a large bucket of stones from one place and drops it in another. A large orange ferry slowly crosses the horizon. A fishing boat bobs gently on the waves.

'And,' says Dilan, looking down at the ground, 'most importantly, my skateboard has gone.'

Chapter 4

'Gordon Bennett! What you wearin'?' says a boy on the oddest bike I've ever seen. He's pointing at Dilan's shorts.

'Surf pants,' says Dilan, staring down at his legs. 'What sort of bike is that?'

'You know – a Chopper – five-speed, see?' The boy fiddles with a large black ball on the end of a chrome stick. He weaves out across the play park and back, the front wheel wobbling from side to side. 'Anyway, you look ridiculous,' he says. 'Surprised your mum let you out like that.' He stops, and climbs off his bike. He's wearing a huge coat with a baggy bum and a fur collar. His trousers stick out at the bottom, and don't reach his shoes.

'Right, yeah,' says Dilan, moving forwards to inspect the bike.

I look around the play park. The rubbish roundabout seems to have been replaced by a wooden spinning thing that moves much more easily. I push it and leap on. It whizzes around at twice the speed of the one that was here before and I actually have to stop it.

I climb off. The play park spins for a moment and I sit

down while the yoghurt finds my stomach again.

'What's your name?' says Dilan.

'What's yours?' says the boy.

'Dilan,' says Dilan.

'Like Bob? That hippy bloke?' says the boy. 'Mine's Dave Dando.' He puts out his right hand.

Dilan stares at it and tries to high-five. Only it doesn't work and they both look a little foolish.

'Like Dando's the surf shop in the high street – is that your dad?' I say.

Dave stares at me blankly. 'My dad's a fireman. How come I haven't seen you two around?' he says, clambering back on his bike and peddling around in an almost circle.

'Oh,' I say, 'we've just moved.'

'Moved to Dunroamin'?' Dave points towards our house.

'Yes. No. Don't know,' says Dilan. 'We're just having a walk. Going to the shop.'

'Don't let me keep you,' says Dave, making an exaggerated gesture along the path.

This is not the way to the shop – at least not the quick way, but we walk on anyway, clanging out of the far side of the play park, and on to the cul-de-sac that joins the estate to the town.

We swing around the corner. Everything here looks much as normal, although there don't seem to be so many cars and the ones that are there are square, old ones. But in very good condition.

'Classics,' says Dilan, pointing at a red shiny car with sheepskin on the steering wheel.

'Where are the satellite dishes? And the trees are tiny.' I say.

'Are they filming something?' says Dilan. 'Perhaps we've wandered onto a film set – or any second now a horde of silent, very hungry mutant jellyfish could emerge from the sea and eat us,' he says, almost cheerfully. 'Cos they've obviously eaten everything else.'

I move closer to him, pulling at the sleeve of his T-shirt, like I used to hang onto Mum's bag when I was little. This new version of Shabbiton is scaring me.

Dilan doesn't brush me away; he grabs my hand back, as if even he might be finding this just a little bit scary.

'Even the bus-stop sign looks different,' I say, gazing upward and thumping into Dilan's side as he stops suddenly.

'That,' says Dilan, 'shouldn't be there.' He points at a collapsed cottage planted right in the middle of the footpath through to the school.

'And look at what's happened to the shop,' I whisper.

We cross the road and stare in the windows. It looks like a time capsule. Old packets of washing powder and biscuits on one side; on the other, comics and magazines with terrible orange and brown lettering. Just to the side of the doorway is a rack of newspapers. The names are familiar, but the headlines don't make any sense.

'General Pinochet, New President of Chile'

'More Power Cuts on the Way'

My eye strays to the date. 2nd July 1974.

Chapter 5

I'm not sure either of us wants to go further, but we don't actually stop each other. We walk on through almost familiar streets to the seafront.

The area around the pier looks very similar to the way it should, except that Henderson's huge car showroom isn't there, nor are the estate agents', or the pound shop, but the baker's is there, and the flower shop, and the newsagent with the buckets and spades, but nothing prepares me for the pier itself.

Where usually there's a boarded-up chippy, here there are two pretty wooden booths, one hanging with buckets and candyfloss and popcorn; the other advertising tickets to events in the Castle Ballroom. *'Dirk Brinsley and the Cherokees . . . Loretta Bacall and her performing chinchillas . . . Live Music Every Night . . . Dancing, Ballroom and Jive, professional teachers and exhibition performers. £1 entry afternoons, £2 evenings. Special event tonite: the finals of the Frank Darnell Competition Cup, 7–11p.m.'* The booths are painted red and gold and look as if they have been every year since they were built. Tall lit-up letters blaze above our heads – CASTLE BALLROOM – and underneath in curly writing: *The Best in the East.*

It's busy too. The normally deserted Shabbiton seafront is buzzing with people, mostly overdressed, clustering around the pier. I'm aware that we look really out of place and pull Dilan back until we're safely hidden in a fishy alley by the arcade.

'I've always thought it would look really skanky, but it doesn't. It's . . .'

'Yes . . .' I say, stepping aside as a collection of women wearing thick make-up bustle past and across the road to the pier. 'Dilan, can we go home now?'

We walk in silence back to the play park. Dave is still trying out turns on his bike. Two other boys are kicking a ball, and a girl's appeared on a space hopper. Three more come in from the other end with long lengths of elastic.

I am probably in a state of shock. I should probably be given a cup of sweet tea and a biscuit. This is how I felt when Mum told us we were moving house, as if it couldn't possibly happen, and again when Granddad moved in with us.

The ground is still ground, but it's clearer than it was before, and ever so slightly threatening. For a moment I imagine millions of microbes squirming under the earth's crust – waiting to spring out and grab our ankles before taking over our minds. Or is it the other people? Are they actually aliens, robots in rubber human suits?

The girl catches sight of Dilan's shorts and giggles.

Dilan frowns but doesn't say anything.

Dave wobbles towards the fence and rests his arms around the supports. 'Back?' he says, slipping a finger up his nose, pulling something out and inspecting it before eating it.

'What's the date today?' I ask, wondering what alien snot tastes like.

'2nd July 1974 – only three more weeks of school,' he says.

'Oh,' says Dilan, nodding his head. 'Of course.'

We head out of the play park and through the houses to the building site. Dilan sits on a pile of blocks, and I join him. We stay silent for a long time, scraping patterns in the dirt, listening to the birds, but neither of us saying anything.

'Try screaming,' I say in the end.

'Why?'

'Because when you're dreaming, you can't shout – you can't call for help.'

Dilan opens his mouth and lets out a shout. A bevy of seagulls flap into the air, circle and land again. He turns and punches me hard on the arm.

'OW! Why'd you do that?'

'Just checking,' he says, 'that you're not dreaming too.'

I rub my arm. 'So – it's not a dream then. Either Earth's been invaded by nice chatty aliens on weird bikes with a lousy fashion sense, or we're in 1974 and we've somehow stepped into the past, through a fridge portal, and are now occupying a parallel time period. Personally, I'd go for the second one as being more likely.'

'Bugg – wake up. We can't have done. It's not possible.'

He's right. Even with my small grasp of history and physics I know that *The Time Machine* and *Doctor Who* are actually fiction. Even if Einstein thought it was theoretically possible to travel in time, he never proved it, and if all the minds at the great universities haven't managed to do it yet, then the likelihood of a 1920s bungalow managing to invent a time machine, unaided, is very, very small. Time travel is far too complicated and unlikely to have been invented by a fridge.

I turn it over and over in my head. 'But, Dilan – what other explanation is there? I mean, is everyone dressing up just to fool us?' I wave at the building site. 'Has someone knocked down the entire estate just to give us a bad afternoon?'

Dilan sighs. He is actually speechless. I'm not sure I've ever known that happen.

'OK,' I say. 'So it happened when we ate the yoghurts . . .'

Dilan doesn't move, just stares straight ahead at the ground.

'Which came from the fridge,' I say.

'Yes,' he says. And then he says. 'Bugg, in 1974 – had they invented skateboards?'

Chapter 6

We stumble back towards the house. I think we both feel that we need to see that fridge again – it's the only thing that links both places – the here place and the other place.

That's when I have an idea.

'We should leave a mark,' I say.

'How do you mean?' asks Dilan.

'I mean, I know we can't possibly be in the past, but something we can see if we get back to now – I mean, then – I mean, 2014.'

'What's not going to change?' he says. 'Assuming of course that we have actually time-travelled, which as we know is impossible.'

'It's got to be something that could survive forty years, without being painted over or washed away.'

I scan the building site. I can't yet make out which houses will be which, but they've already put the fire hydrants in next to little metal hinged covers set into what will be the road. I open the nearest cover. Beside the thing for turning the water on and off there's plenty of room.

'Have you got anything we could hide in there?' I ask,

reaching into my pockets. I find an elastic band, a five-pence piece dated 1999 and some fluff.

Dilan pulls out two fused sherbet lemons and a plastic book token that Aunty Sarah gave him for Christmas. 'It's still got 79p on it,' he says. 'I'm not sure I want to leave it.'

'But if it's still there when we reach now – I mean, normal time,' I say, 'you can use it then.'

Dilan furrows his forehead as if he's trying to make sense of what I've just said. It makes perfect sense to me, but then I spend hours at night trying to work out looping sci-fi plots so that I don't think about the monsters that undoubtedly live in the washing machine. I'm used to time travel – virtually.

I also know the fundamental rule. You mustn't fiddle with anything from the past, because it could massively affect the future. All time travellers must know this. I also know that it's possible to end up not having been born and that we must be REALLY careful.

'Suppose there's a fire in the meantime – I mean, the firemen might find my card and throw it away?'

'We'll hide it,' I say. 'Anyway, it's only 79p.'

The house is quiet. We duck under the living room window and stop outside the kitchen door, listening. The door's still open and I can actually see the empty yoghurt pots on the side.

We move into the doorway. The blue-painted doorway that should be green; our feet nearly on the blue and cream-tiled floor that should be brown.

Dilan points at the yoghurt pots on the side.

I point to the fridge. The fridge is humming, singing, like it did at home. We tiptoe into the kitchen and pull the door open. The fridge sighs and rattles, shaking itself slightly while I reach in and grab two yoghurts.

Dilan snatches the empty ones with spoons from the side and we duck back outside and crouch beneath the scrawny little tree.

'They're different,' he whispers. 'They're like modern ones.'

I look down at the pots in my hands. As before, they have indistinct fruit – I can't totally identify the flavour – they could be peach or pear, but they have thin peely lids and plastic containers. On the side they have a proper date: 2nd July 2014. I point at it.

Dilan frowns, rips off the top and plunges the spoon into the pale orange contents. He brings out a huge glob and rams it in his mouth. 'I don't care – I just want to get back home.'

I peel back the lid and taste the yoghurt. It's just as delicious as before, so it's easy to jam the whole lot into my mouth and lick out the inside.

'Bugg.' Dilan nudges my arm. 'Look.'

But I hear it first. The murmur of the estate. Cars, machines, voices, radios, all setting up a hum that I'd never noticed in the ordinary world before. I open my eyes; we're crouched under the apple tree. It hangs over us, heavy with fruit, buzzing with insects and birds.

'Oh, there you are,' says Mum, sticking her head around the door. 'Can someone look after Granddad? Give him something to eat – I've got a Historical Society Meeting and your dad's not back from work yet.' She slams the back door and we hear her go round to the front, followed by the crash of a car door closing and then the sound of the engine starting up.

Dilan sits examining the yoghurt pot. I do the same. I think there's too much to say for either of us to try.

'Book token?' says Dilan.

'Yes,' I say, not moving.

'I don't think I want to find out if it's there – or if it's not there,' he says, staring at the back of his hand.

'I'll go and see Granddad,' I say in the end, taking my yoghurt pot and dumping it in the bin.

'Good idea,' says Dilan, bunging the other three into the sink.

I hear Granddad before I see him.

'*De dum, de dum, de ta ta ta – de dum, de dum, de ta ta ta . . .*'

I go through to the living room. It's boiling. Granddad's got the electric bar fire on, and the evening sun is streaming through the conservatory roof, bringing everything up to about a million degrees.

'See,' Granddad says, pointing at the telly. 'They were a couple. *De dum, de dum, de ta ta ta . . .*'

I agree, two people on the screen dancing together, undoubtedly a couple.

'Look at that,' he points.

'What am I looking at?' I say.

'The way he dances,' Granddad struggles to his feet,

grabbing a rolled-up rug that's leaning against the wall. 'See?' Granddad grips the body of the rug with his left arm, and sticks his right arm out, holding the fringe with his fingertips. He takes two paces. '*De ta, de ta, de ta ba ba* – he danced like that.'

I suspect I'm missing the finer points.

Granddad continues to demonstrate, blundering around the sitting room, knocking things off tables. I rescue a pile of DVDs and a lamp before he drops the rug and slumps back onto the sofa. 'He was a great dancer, one of the very best. Went on to present shows on the telly.' Granddad turns up the volume and leans forward to hear the judge's comments. 'He used to dance here, you know, on special exhibition nights.' He sighs and rubs his eyes, as if he's got grit in them. 'That was before the beautiful pier burned down, not long after your gran died and your dad was just a little'un . . .'

He sniffs. 'Young once, you know. Back then, the Castle Ballroom was a gem. Me and it, in the prime of life – and look at us now. Two old wrecks. We were young once, you know,' he says, as if he's never said it before.

'Yes, Granddad,' I say, staring at the shapes whirling on the screen, thinking of the pier Dilan and I saw half an hour and forty years ago. 'I know you were, once. I just wonder what happened to you both.'

I'm in bed now, but I'm not going to go to sleep in a hurry. Dilan and I ate noodles with Granddad on the sofa before Dad came back and cooked real food. We ate our proper supper around the table, but Granddad didn't join us. 'Happy with this, thanks,' he said, slurping a cup of soup.

'Dad,' I'd said at supper, 'do you think time travel will ever be possible?'

Dilan choked on his cabbage.

But Dad was shaking his head. 'You read too much science fiction. It might be, but then, the transporters from *Star Trek*'ll probably come first. More stew? Or are you off to bed?'

Granddad's dance music thumps through the floor. Modern tunes. He must be watching live TV, and it keeps me awake so that even though I'm ridiculously tired I can't get to sleep. When I do nearly fall asleep, Mum clanking about on the landing pulls me awake and then I just can't stop thinking about this afternoon. The only explanation is that we time-travelled. That we went back into the past, although surely that's totally impossible. Otherwise we had a dream or something – both of us at the same time, drugged by the yoghurt and taken into a sleeping state. I think about Dave Dando and I wonder if he'd remember us, and I think about Dilan's book token – would it still be there, and if it was, what would that prove?

And then I think that perhaps the best way to prove it would be to put something from now, that we could find then. A piece of twenty-first-century life, or even just a coin, that would prove that we came from the future.

But will we ever find 'then' again?

Was it just a fluke? Or were we guided by the fridge? Does the fridge know what's happening?

Is the fridge actually a life form?

Does it have a brain?

Or is there a giant metallic fungus and the fridge is a tiny growth on the top: the thing we can see only the tip of the iceberg? Maybe the whole town is built on a giant time-travelling piece of metal, activated by sea mist and candyfloss, and it's trying to trap us into altering time, because of some evil-genius life plan it has.

Eventually my brain implodes and I fall asleep.

Chapter 7

'*Oh, don't disheeve me . . .*'

It's Granddad's quavery voice, singing up the stairs.

'*. . . oh, never leave me . . .*'

I sit bolt upright. I grope for the alarm clock. Eight forty-five.

Eight forty-five?

School started five minutes ago.

What?

I throw on my school uniform and charge out of the door, running into Dilan's bedroom and kicking him. 'Get up!' I shout, and slide down the stairs, arriving breathless at the bottom.

Granddad's at the foot of the stairs, his dressing gown all tangled and inside out. It doesn't seem to bother him; he's serenading the Christmas edition of the *Radio Times*. 'Granddad,' I say, pulling the dressing gown gently from his shoulders and shaking all the crumbs out.

'Y' movver's not 'ere,' he mumbles to Father Christmas. 'Can't find me front teef.' I help him back on with the dressing gown. He starts singing again. '*How could you use a poor maiden so?*' It takes an age to get his arms into the holes and I watch the hall clock creep around to five past nine.

'Havvn't had bekfass,' he says eventually, as an avalanche of old tissues cascades from his pocket.

I hold my breath, pick them up with my extreme fingertips and carry them to the bin in the kitchen.

The fridge hums. I look across at it. It's developed a plastic O.

ACTO.

Otherwise everything's quiet, even deserted. Last night's plates sit on the side, they haven't even made it into the dishwasher. The table's scattered with crumbs, the teapot's cold.

'See,' whistles Granddad through his gums. 'No-un – ad look at a 'ime.' He points to the clock. It's nearly quarter past. 'Ugry – cud ave a yoghurt?'

'No!' I say, leaping to block the fridge door. I do not like the idea of Granddad wandering around in the early 1970s – especially not in that dressing gown. 'Stay here, we'll have something else for breakfast. I'll find your teeth.'

Granddad sleeps in what is probably supposed to be a study. It's a boiling-hot room built onto the side of the living room, heaped with more things to make it hot, like electric blankets and pink eiderdowns that came from his old house and smell of mice.

Stumbling over the huge collection of slippers with chunks cut out of them to accommodate his bunions, I finally find a light switch.

I've not been in here much since Granddad moved in. He's been nesting. His old piano, formerly just covered in dust, has an array of tarnished silver trophies and a pair of ancient cracked-leather dancing shoes placed on the top. He obviously doesn't like cupboards, because his clothes are arranged on hangers dangling from the picture rail. There're a few ancient cardigans, but mostly black suits, smart ones, thin ones, some with bow ties looped over the hanger.

By his bed, his chest of drawers is equally cluttered. I brush aside the photo frames until I find a glass.

Inside the glass, suspended in something that might or might not be water, are his front teeth.

'Here you are, Granddad,' I say – waving the glass at him. He takes it and peers closely at the pink and white teeth floating inside. I realise that he doesn't have his glasses on.

'Blesh you, Bugg,' he says, holding them up in the air and letting them drip on the carpet before cramming them into his mouth.

I wade back into his room and fumble around on the chest of drawers. His glasses are there, draped over the corner of one of the photos. I pick it up and look. It's a man and woman dancing. He's wearing a black suit, a white shirt, a bow tie. She's got a peachy-pink dress with a huge feathery skirt, and although the photo's faded and cracked, I can make out chandeliers and pale green flocked wallpaper. At the bottom it says: *To Arnold – hoping to make this victory the first of many, Doreen*. Arnold is Granddad's name. I examine the photo – I suppose the face is Granddad's, but you'd hardly know that the shambling thing in the kitchen and the man in the photo were remotely related.

Back in the kitchen, I hand Granddad his glasses, reach into the cupboard for a bowl and the cornflakes, and that's when I spot the yoghurt pots on the side.

Two of them, empty. Spoons sticking out of the top, and not the ones that we ate yesterday. Two more yoghurt pots.

Chapter 8

Dilan and I sit with Granddad while we all eat bowls of cereal. I'm in the room, but my mind's elsewhere.

Gone. They've gone, and worse than that, they've left us with Granddad. I glance over at the yoghurt pots. They look different from the ones that Dilan and I tried yesterday. More cone-shaped. I wonder if they've gone back to 1974 – or even further. Perhaps they're meeting Dave Dando. And then an awful thought jumps into my mind. Perhaps Dad's meeting himself – as a baby.

I don't know what happens if you meet yourself. In all the books I've ever read it's meant instant death, or sparks, or one of you has to disappear.

I imagine Dad leaning over the side of a pram and both he and the baby melting into each other.

He might end up as some hideous hybrid. Half man, half baby.

He wouldn't stand a chance.

I look back at Granddad. He's managed to fleck globs of gloopy food down his pyjama top. If Mum or Dad were here, they'd whisk it off him and bung it in the washing machine, but I don't feel able to do that, so I pass him a tissue and point at the slobber and hope for the best.

When we finally leave for school, the bus doesn't come for ages. We wait at the bus stop and neither of us says the thing that's hanging over us. Neither of us mentions the awful possibility that our parents might be lost in time. Instead Dilan listens to his iPod and fiddles with his phone.

'Weird,' he says. 'I've got loads of random texts. They must have come through yesterday – I just didn't notice.'

'Who from?' I say, hoping it could be Mum and Dad.

'Me,' he says. 'They're from me. I'm telling myself what's going to be for lunch – what?'

I scrape lichen from the glass, worried.

By the time we arrive it's nearly break time and we have to explain ourselves.

The school secretary, Miss Golightly, is behind her desk, picking peanut brittle out of her teeth. She thinks we don't know that she eats all the time, but we do, and it's fairly obviously peanut brittle because the wrappers overflow from the bin beside the door . . . and because she's absolutely enormous.

'Bugg, Dilan – what happened to you? I was just going to ring home.' She's a got a deep warm hot-chocolate voice. It makes her difficult to resist.

'Mum and Dad—' starts Dilan, but I cut him off. I know what he's going to say, but he shouldn't – not yet.

'The alarm didn't go off, sorry, and then there was a bit of trouble with Granddad,' I say.

'Oh – dear Arnold.' Her face creases into a look of genuine

sorrow. 'How is he – any better?'

I think about Granddad dancing with the *Radio Times*. 'Much the same thanks, Miss Golightly.'

She heaves a sigh. 'Such a shame, such a shame – and to think what could have been if things had been different.' She sighs again and flaps her hands at us. 'Off to break – and then into class.'

'Why did you cut me off?' asks Dilan as we go down the corridor.

'Because we mustn't tell anyone that Mum and Dad have disappeared. They'll send the social services, and take us away, and then we'll never be able to get Mum and Dad back.'

Dilan looks at me. 'Do you really think . . . ?'

'I do,' I say.

Dilan sighs, gloomily. 'I reckon you're wrong,' he says, scratching his head. 'Anyway – you never know, they might be back already.'

I sit in maths calculating the age that Mum and Dad would be now, if they got stuck in 1974 and by some miracle Dad didn't meet himself. I think that Dad would be eighty-six and Mum would be seventy-five. Where would they live? How would they live? Would they even know that they'd travelled in time or would they think everyone had suddenly got rid of all the cars and knocked down the housing estate?

'Bugg – in this equation – what is the nth term?'

I stare blankly at the board and feel sick. I'm losing touch with reality.

English is agony. We're doing *Macbeth*. I start to worry about Mum and Dad going back to Shakespeare's time. Or even the Stone Age. They'd never survive. Mum has to have a cup of tea with fresh milk every day, and Dad can't move before he's read the newspaper, and they'd never understand what anyone was saying to them. All those grunts.

In geography we all set out into the town with clipboards. For the first time I notice just how dismal the seafront is. It's all battered plywood and skanky posters, broken palm trees with piles of windblown sand clustered around their roots. It's as if Henderson's car showroom is so big and so shiny it's sucked all the life out of everything around it. The pier itself is a set of posts stuck with seaweed near the shore, and the faintest frame of rusted metal further out at sea. I can still make out the bottoms of the flag poles, but otherwise it's just Henderson's overflow car park full of gleaming cars.

At the end of the day I go to drama club. Miss Swanson asks us all to trust each other. We take it in turns to blunder around with our eyes closed, trusting and crashing into radiators. My partner is an irritatingly bouncy girl called Lorna, who's only recently moved into my class and whose mum runs the shop. The same shop we saw in 1974. She was at another school, but I reckon they moved her because she's so irritating. She just does stuff – like saying things when people shouldn't, and asking teachers things that would be better left alone. Last week she told the dinner ladies that the dinners were disgusting and that they shouldn't overcook everything. She's right, everything is overcooked, but you shouldn't say anything about it. It's just the way it is. The worst thing is that I think she likes me: she keeps appearing at my elbow, even though I never hear her coming and it makes me jump.

I'm supposed to be nice to her, because Mum says we need to be nice to her. This is not really a sufficient reason, but I try not to guide her into the wall.

But I'm not really concentrating on the drama class. I'm worrying about Granddad getting peckish, helping himself to a yoghurt and going back to the Second World War, when Shabbiton was covered in barbed wire and anti-aircraft guns.

It would finish him off.

Lorna leads me into the radiator for the third time. 'Ow!' I say, as I bang my knee.

'Whoops – sorree,' she says. 'Wasn't thinking.'

I don't think she's actually deliberately stupid, but it doesn't make me want to be her partner.

'Blindfolds off!' calls Miss Swanson.

I rub my eyes and glance up at the clock. Four o'clock. That means Mum should be picking me up any minute.

'Now, everyone, before the end of the session, can we try the ultimate trust game?' Miss Swanson claps her hands. 'Lorna, stand on this chair, would you?'

Lorna springs over and climbs onto the chair, swinging her arms, all keen and . . . ugh.

'Now, everyone else, we have to make Lorna feel safe enough to throw herself forward into our arms. So gather round and let's put our arms out, to make a springy bed for her.'

We move together. There are only eight of us, but I suppose Lorna doesn't weigh much. 'Ready?' Miss Swanson gazes up at Lorna.

'You mean I just throw myself forward on your arms?' says Lorna.

Miss Swanson grins and nods. 'Yes – you'll be perfectly safe.'

'OK,' says Lorna, bending her knees, ready for a dive, before launching herself right over our arms and onto the gym floor.

Chapter 9

Lorna's nosebleed doesn't stop for ages.

'I'm s'posed to be cubbing home wiv you,' she says through the bloody tissue.

'Really?' I say.

'Yes, my mum spoke to your mum.'

'Oh –' I say.

But my mum doesn't come. Dilan's already gone home, presumably on the bus, and I didn't bring enough money for the bus fare home, certainly not enough for me and blood-stained Lorna.

At five, Miss Golightly takes pity on us and says, 'I know I shouldn't, but I'll run you back, dears.'

So we cram into her miniature car, really designed for two ordinary-sized people, not one peanut brittle addict and two medium children, and she drives us scarily fast through the streets before juddering to a breathless halt at the back of a traffic queue. We wait for an enormous removal van to back into the drive of a massive house.

Miss Golightly sighs, tapping her fingers on the dashboard. 'The Hendersons, moving house again. Apparently that house has got its own cinema.'

'And a swimming pool,' says Lorna.

I watch two removal men struggle up the steps with a green and gold chandelier modelled on the monuments of Europe. One of the Eiffel Towers jams in the doorway, and the little nodule on the top pings off.

'The problem with that lot,' says Miss Golightly, 'is that they've no taste and too much money,' She slaps her hand over her mouth. 'Shh – I never said that. Most unprofessional.'

'But you're right,' says Lorna. 'No manners either. Mum told Eddie Henderson he wasn't welcome in the shop because he was so rude.'

'Really?' says Mrs Golightly. 'I always thought Mrs Henderson was rather nice.'

I try to picture what they even look like. All fairly enormous, as I remember. Like their houses and cars.

'Oh, I think she's OK. It's Eddie really. He's won the lottery twice, you know. Mum says the chances of that are something like 28 million to one.'

'Well, good luck to them,' says Miss Golightly, slamming her foot down on the accelerator and sending us flat against the seat back.

As we whizz past Dando's Surf Shack I peer in past the baseball caps and skates to see if I can see Dave Dando – but if the overweight middle-aged man behind the counter is Dave, I'd have been hard pushed to identify him as the boy on the bike.

'There,' says Miss Golightly, screeching to a halt outside

our house. 'Is your Granddad in?' she asks.

'He's always in,' I say, before I realise that I don't want Miss Golightly to come inside and see last night's dinner scattered across the kitchen. 'But he might be asleep.'

'Jolly good,' she says, unsticking herself from the driver's seat and swinging past me towards the front door.

'Can I come?' asks Lorna, still holding most of a loo roll against her nose.

'Um,' I say, but she's already in the house.

I rush through to find Miss Golightly holding Granddad's hand. He's sitting on the sofa, gazing at the telly – I'm not sure he's even noticed her. She looks as if she might cry, but I'm afraid I don't care, I'm just grateful to find him there and not back in the Bronze Age.

'Who's that?' asks Lorna.

I don't answer, just pull the door shut so that Miss Golightly and Granddad can have a little time together.

'Why are you called Bugg?' asks Lorna, sliding into the kitchen.

'It's short for Jitterbug,' I say, looking at the chaos that was once our kitchen. Granddad must have made his own lunch. It seems to have been tuna and instant custard.

'Litterbug?' says Lorna beside me, agape. Then, 'Whoa . . . what a mess!'

'No, Jitterbug,' I say. 'It's a dance. Haven't you got to get home?'

'Not really,' she says. 'Mum's in the shop, I could hang around. What about Dilan?'

'It's a dance too, a folk dance. And actually, you can't

hang around. You see it's . . .' I fumble around desperately for an excuse. 'It's Dad's deadly snake society night. We can't have anyone else here, it might upset them.'

Lorna blinks excitedly. 'Really? I love deadly snakes.'

'And they bring their scorpions,' I say.

Lorna's eyes light up.

'And crabs – they quite often have giant crabs.'

'Fantastic. Cool,' she says.

'But you have to leave – they won't like it if you stay. Some of the snake fanciers have really bad tempers.'

'O–K,' she says, suspiciously easily. 'I'll go.'

Chapter 10

Miss Golightly only stays a little longer. When she leaves, she brushes tears from her eyes. 'So sad,' she says. 'So sad.' I thank her for the lift, push the door shut behind her and rush into the kitchen.

I don't actually know how you're supposed to tidy a kitchen, so I bung everything in the dishwasher and put it on extra hot and extra long and then sweep all the crumby stuff into a pile on the countertop. This, I have no idea how to deal with.

I stare at the fridge. 'It's your fault,' I say out loud. It hums, then gurgles. I rearrange the letters. COAT. OCAT. TACO. I'd swear it was laughing at me. I turn my back to study the empty yoghurt pots on the side.

'I looked,' says Dilan, arriving at my side, carrying his skateboard. 'I couldn't make out the numbers.'

'Where have you been?' I ask.

'Walked,' he said. 'Back through the estate, and look what I found.' He flicks up the book token that we hid. 'Proof.'

I turn it over in my hand. 'It's sort of proof. But we might have put it there recently, found it now, and just have been under some kind of hallucination.'

'But what about these?' Dilan points at the yoghurt pots. 'Where have Mum and Dad gone if they haven't taken a spin through time?'

'I thought,' I say, 'you said time travel was my delusion – that it was impossible.'

He leans over to fiddle with his trainer. 'That was yesterday. Today I think time travel is perfectly possible, and I'm ready to argue it out with anyone. Anyway, I looked it up on the Internet. Apparently there could be something called a traversable wormhole. No one's proved they can't exist . . .'

I take another look at the pots, and then open the fridge. Six more yoghurts that I don't remember seeing before are lined up at the top. They actually look as if they've shoved the butter and lettuce to one side. They're different from the pots that we ate yesterday – they're cone-shaped, like Mum's and Dad's.

'Dilan, look,' I say, standing back from the door.

He springs to his feet, grabs one and examines it.

'I can't find a date,' he says. 'But they look . . . older.'

The kitchen door opens, and Granddad shuffles in. He looks a mess, blobs of food down his front and he hasn't shaved, but he's singing. '*Early one mo-or-ning, just as the sun was* . . . Anything to eat?' he says, peering in the bread bin.

'I'll make you some toast,' I say.

'Oh – I fancy a yoghurt. Look at that! Haven't seen one like that since – oooh – ages.' Granddad grabs one of the yoghurts from the fridge.

'Oh no, Granddad,' says Dilan. 'I think Mum's keeping those for something.'

Granddad pauses. A droplet forms between his nostrils, stretches and plunges to the ground. For a moment he looks as if he's going to say something, but he just nods, puts down the yoghurt and turns back to the loaf of bread, gazing at it as if he's no idea what it is.

'We should have won the paso doble ,' he says and shuffles out of the door.

We stare at his back as he drops heavily onto the sofa cushions and presses the buttons on the remote control.

'We should look for Mum and Dad,' says Dilan. 'In time.' He rummages in the cutlery basket for a teaspoon and finds three more plastic letters. *I*, *U* and *N*. He sticks them on the fridge door.

COTAINU.

'But we can't leave Granddad,' I say, scraping butter onto Granddad's toast and cutting it into fingers. 'Look at him! After one day on his own he's a mess. The only food he can prepare for himself is noodles.'

Dilan wrenches open the cupboard over the kettle where Mum keeps the noodles. It's distressingly empty. 'He must have eaten them all today,' he says, peering in the bin. 'Yup – he did.'

I take Granddad his toast. He's watching a black and white film. There's a man dancing and singing. Granddad's humming along and his feet are twitching.

'Great film this, Bugg,' he says. '*Top Hat*. Ginger Rogers

always said she had to do everything Fred Astaire did, but backwards in high heels.' He waves at the screen, tipping the plate so that the toast barely clings on. 'Don't see dancing like that any more. Everyone could dance when I was young.' He turns to look at me. 'I was young once. Best in the East, you know.'

'OK, Granddad,' I say. 'Just going to nip out and buy you some noodles.'

Dilan butts in. 'You haven't got any money, have you, Granddad?'

Granddad wobbles to his feet. The toast gives up and slides to the floor, joining some banana skins that Granddad dropped earlier. He reaches into the pockets of his dressing gown and plucks out two small handfuls of coins.

He reaches out towards me and I cup my hands underneath. Like the claw machine in the amusement arcade, he drops the coins into my hands. Among them is a ten-pound note. I bundle it all into my pockets.

Chapter 11

We head towards the shop. Dilan bobs along beside me on his skateboard. His jeans hang under his bum and he keeps on having to stop to pull them up.

The third time it happens I stand and wait on the pavement.

'Sorree,' he says. 'It's just I prefer these trousers.'

The shop's empty. We stick fifteen packets of instant noodles into a basket and wait for someone to appear at the counter. It's Lorna. She puts something that strikes me as alive into her cardigan pocket.

'So, why are you and Dilan named after stupid dances then?'

I'm going to ignore it, but Dilan says, 'Granddad's obsessed with dance, and Mum and Dad agreed. I think they hoped one of us would dance.' He swings a pirouette, knocking a pyramid of tinned beans to the floor. 'Ooops.' We scrabble to pick the cans up.

'Why are you called Lorna?'

'Dunno.' Lorna shrugs and starts to scan the noodles into the till.

Her mum appears from the back room. 'More noodles?

Your mum bought the shop out last week. Don't tell me your Granddad's already got through them all!'

'N—' says Dilan.

'Hwwa,' I say, hoping that she won't ask any more questions.

We bung the noodles mainly into my pockets but some have to go into Dilan's stupid trousers. About two doors down the road, we have to stop and pick up all the packets that have fallen out of his pockets. When I look up from rearranging the packets, Lorna's standing there.

'Hello,' she says. 'Why d'you need all these? And where's your mum?'

We rustle a little further down the pavement and have to stop again. Lorna fumbles in her pocket and produces a blue carrier bag, which she holds out with one hand. I notice that she keeps her other hand in her cardigan pocket as if something's trying to get out.

'We need them for Granddad,' says Dilan, grabbing her bag and dropping the noodles in.

'Yes,' I say. 'Granddad.'

'Can I come back with you?' she says, picking a last piece of dried blood from her nose. 'I'll go when the snake fanciers arrive.'

'Snake fanciers?' says Dilan. 'What snake fanciers?'

'You know,' I say quickly. 'Dad's friends, with the scorpions.' I nudge Dilan and he goes quiet, but with a puzzled look on his face.

Lorna follows us right into the kitchen and stands by the fridge as we load the noodles into the cupboard. 'I'll have the bag back,' she says. 'They're useful in the shop.' She twists it into a rope, wrapping it around her fingers like a blue snake. She stares about at the mess. 'Oh my word! I've just worked it out: your mum and dad have gone, haven't they?' she says. 'You're going to live on noodles, aren't you? Where've they gone? Have they run away? That is sooooo exciting.'

'No,' I say.

'Yes,' says Dilan.

I look at the floor. Dilan opens the fridge door.

'You wouldn't believe us,' I mutter.

'What wouldn't I believe?' asks Lorna, fiddling with the thing in her pocket again.

'Huh?' says Dilan, peering into the fridge. 'There are seven now.' He points at the yoghurts.

'What does that mean?' says Lorna, stuffing the carrier bag into her pocket, pushing past and grabbing the nearest pot.

'Don't,' I whisper as she runs her fingers over the foil.

'Don't what?' she says, peeling back the lid and peering inside.

'Don't eat it,' I say. 'Please.'

'Why not?'

I glance at Dilan. He rearranges the yoghurts in the fridge.

'What's that thing in your pocket?' I ask Lorna, desperate to change the subject.

'This?' She reaches into her cardigan. 'Did you hear that, Coleridge? They want to meet you.' She pulls out something furry.

'What,' asks Dilan, 'is that?'

'It's a gerbil. Haven't you seen one before?' Nestled in her palm is a little rat-like thing with a long tail. 'Gerbils are amazing. They reproduce really fast. You have to be careful with them, make sure you don't mix males and females. They're clever, and they're really tough too, like me.' She points at the yoghurt. 'So what happens if I eat it?'

'Weird things happen,' I say in the end.

Lorna raises her eyebrows. 'Like what?'

'We think . . . that you sort of . . . time . . . thing.'

'Bugg!' snaps Dilan. 'Don't.'

'But she won't go away. We have to, otherwise we're not going to be able to . . . you know.'

'Time what?' says Lorna, sticking the gerbil back into her cardigan and peering into the yoghurt pot, her finger poised over the goo inside. 'Tell me, or I'll eat it.'

Dilan sighs. 'Time-travel.'

'You're right. I don't believe you,' she says staring into the pot. 'Where's the machine? You can't time-travel without a machine.'

I tap the door of the fridge. 'Here,' I say. 'It seems to make the yoghurts.'

Lorna's jaw drops and she stares at the old yellowed door. 'That is so lame,' she says. 'Everyone knows you need a machine. A proper one, made by a mad scientist. You know, a bloke in a white coat.'

Dilan taps the fridge. 'How do we know this wasn't made by a mad scientist – either in the future – or the past?'

'What? That is so . . . unlikely.'

I shake my head. 'Whatever. The thing is, these –' I hold

up the empty yoghurt pots – 'were eaten by our parents, who have disappeared. And, as they haven't come back, and maybe don't know how to, we're off to find them. But – in case it takes longer – we're leaving Granddad with some instant noodles because that's the only food he can prepare.'

Chapter 12

Lorna agrees to stay and keep an eye on Granddad. Her gerbil squirms and squeaks in her pocket and I can't help worrying about it.

'Couldn't you take it home first?'

'Don't be ridiculous, Bugg.'

'It's just that it . . .' I begin. Dilan gives me a look close to despair.

Lorna pops some bubblegum into her mouth and chews. She blows a bubble that pops in front of her face. 'Get on with it then,' she says.

I must look anxious because Dilan slaps me between the shoulder blades, as if he's shifting my thoughts. 'Cheer up,' he says. 'It could be worse.'

I don't know how.

While she's waiting for us, Lorna fiddles with the letters on the fridge. TOUCAIN. INCOTUA. U ACTION. 'Oooh, look, a proper anagram. I love those. I do them in the leftover papers.'

U Action? Is the fridge telling us something?

'Come on,' says Dilan, shaking my arm. 'Ready?' He hands

me a yoghurt identical to the empty ones that Mum and Dad ate, and a spoon. Lorna's gawping, obviously expecting some kind of film-type CGI moment, involving bright lights, coloured smoke and magic. I peel off the lid of the pot, this time keeping my eyes on hers. I want to know what happens, at what point we move from now . . . to then.

'How does it taste?' she asks.

'Like good yoghurt,' I say.

'How much have you eaten?'

I look down into the pot, half gone. When I look up, Lorna's not entirely there; it's as if she's a ghost. Her lips are moving but I can't hear what she's saying. I glance over to Dilan. He and the fridge haven't gone sketchy, and for a moment I get the impression of someone else sharing the space, a boy, but he fades, and then it takes a second for the kitchen to solidify.

'Whoa,' mutters Dilan. He's looking around.

'Did you see that?' I ask. 'Someone else in the wobbly bit?'

'No,' he says. 'Whoa – this is so whoa.'

Whoa indeed. We *are* standing in the kitchen. But not the kitchen as I've ever seen it. The fridge is there, white and shiny, practically brand new. Where the countertop should be is a green-painted set of shelves, next to them a huge deep china sink, and on the far side another green-painted thing that might be a countertop.

On the table behind us is a copy of the *Shabbiton Gazette*. Dilan grabs it, turns to the front page and squeaks, '1969.'

I glance towards the sitting room door. This time it's made of spotted glass, and I can see a shape on the other side that could be a person slumped on a sofa.

I tilt my head towards the back door and we slip out into the garden. There is no apple tree. Absolutely no sign of it. Instead, a boring green bush. The garden is surrounded by hedges, and we run through the gateway, and find nothing but fields.

We stop, both staring at a small footpath winding towards the town, into the mist.

Dilan sighs. 'We could just go back,' he says. 'Wait and see what happens.'

I look back at the house and on towards the town again. 'Mum and Dad are out here somewhere. We need to find them, we can't look after Granddad on our own forever.'

The fields are quick to cross. Bees buzz in the hedgerows, and seagulls wheel overhead. It's almost normal, except that it isn't. It's pretty, green, quiet. Like a film.

A child runs past us, flying a kite, her mother behind, pushing an enormous pram with a huge parasol on the top. 'Evening,' says the woman, her face falling when she sees Dilan's under-bum jeans.

I smile at her. I've no idea if I'm supposed to say, 'Evening,' back, so I mumble something under my breath.

'This must be where the play park should be,' says Dilan, stopping at the edge of the last field. 'That must be Bramble Way, and over there, Cowslip Avenue.' He points to a group of grazing sheep chomping their way through the daisies.

'Hey!' A voice makes me turn and I see Lorna heading towards us, along the path. 'Wait for me.'

'I knew we couldn't trust her,' mutters Dilan.

'That was wicked! I saw you go, it was fantastic!' she calls, trotting through the grass. 'The weirdest thing ever.'

'I thought you were going to stay with Granddad,' I say.

Lorna shrugs. 'Sorreee. I couldn't resist it. And, wow! Am I glad! I mean – where are we? When are we?' She sniffs the air, like some sort of excited rabbit.

'1969,' says Dilan wearily.

'Wow,' she says again, reaching into her pocket and pulling out the gerbil. 'Did you hear that, Coleridge? We've time-travelled.'

'How come he time-travelled?' I ask. 'Did he eat the yoghurt?'

Lorna blinks. 'No, silly, he was in my pocket. All of me time-travelled: my socks, my hair, my head. Duh.'

'Well, you're not supposed to be with us,' I say. 'You promised.'

'Did I?' Lorna sniffs.

'You did,' says Dilan.

Lorna drags her toe through the dust, drawing a line. 'But now I'm here . . .'

'Oh, all right,' says Dilan, glancing at me.

'So long as you don't fiddle with anything or touch anything or do anything that might change the past,' I say. 'And so long as that gerbil doesn't either.'

''K,' says Lorna, picking a buttercup.

I look at the buttercup.

'What? Even this?' she says. 'How can a buttercup change history?'

I can't think how a buttercup could possibly change

history, but I keep my face grim. 'Even a buttercup. Don't pick one. Don't even think about picking one.'

We walk into the edge of town. It's familiar, but not. There are hardly any cars, hardly any people. There seem to be more trees, and all the houses have proper front gardens with painted fences. A man strolls past with a dog on a lead. A shiny white car roars down the road, peeping its horn. It looks like Toytown.

'Where would your mum and dad go?' asks Lorna, her voice echoing in the empty streets.

We don't answer. Personally I'm thinking the pier would be a good place to start. It's not burned-out, and apart from anything else, I'd like to see inside it when it looked good. We weave through town until we're standing on the seafront.

'Whoa!' squeals Lorna. 'That is a-maze-ing! It's like something out of the past – so shiny – so smart! Can we go in?'

I'm vaguely irritated that we both want to do the same thing, but I manage not to say anything.

We look up at the posters: '*6d Entry Afternoons. 1s Evenings.*'

'If we want to get in, we need 6d. What's 6d?' asks Dilan.

'Six old pennies,' says Lorna. 'We've got loads back at the shop.'

'Back in the twenty-first century,' I say, reaching my hand into the change that Granddad gave us, pulling up a collection of familiar and unfamiliar coins.

'Those,' says Lorna, jabbing at the coins. 'That's a threepenny piece. Have you got six? That's what we need.'

We haven't, we've only got one. We look pitifully at the man behind the desk.

''Op it. If you can't pay, you can't come in.' We loiter. 'Go on, skat,' he barks, and we step back to stand on the deserted street.

'Mum and Dad wouldn't have had any money,' says Dilan. 'Not the right money, so they're probably not on the pier. Let's look somewhere else.'

'Where else?' I say. Although there are shops, they're all closed. Two dark pubs with smoky windows belch beer smells and cigarette smoke; they don't look like the kinds of places Mum and Dad would go. I walk to the railings overlooking the beach. Seagulls circle overhead, and some children are building a sandcastle. The ballroom music spills along the seafront, jaunty and inviting. 'They have to be in there,' I say. 'We'll just have to find a way in.'

Chapter 13

It's Lorna who suggests sneaking up the fire escape. I'm not mad about the barnacles or the green slimy weed that cling to the rusting metal ladder. They look far too much like something from a special-effects department, something alien and toxic.

We climb onto the pier and find ourselves on the sea end of the ballroom. There's no one here, just seagull poo and the remains of an old carousel.

'Now what?' asks Dilan.

'We go into the ballroom,' says Lorna.

'How?' I ask.

'Like this,' she says, marching in through a door painted with the words 'NO ENTRY'.

I rush in behind her and stand, blinking in the dark. Dilan shuffles in beside me, and we wait for our eyes to adjust. Shapes emerge from the gloom.

Almost the first thing that comes into focus is an enormous glitter ball hanging from the ceiling. As each shard of light bounces from the revolving ball, it catches on the figures flitting across the dance floor. Men in suits steer women in feathery multicoloured dresses back and forth in poses just short of agony. They glide over a gleaming wooden floor encircled by golden chairs with golden cushions. Ornate golden figurines holding harps and horns decorate the walls and ceiling, against a background of pale-green flock wallpaper. I glance back to the dance floor. One particular couple catches my eye. The man looks like Dad, except he doesn't quite – in the same way he looks like Granddad, but a different Granddad, one that's inflated and full of energy, and the young woman in his arms is definitely not Mum; she reminds me of someone else but I can't think who.

I sink to the ground underneath the rows of banked seats, watching the dance floor between a pair of large, baggy-stockinged, elderly ankles.

The dancers swing into what I recognise as a foxtrot, and I follow the Granddad/Dad man skimming through the moves, his feet barely seeming to touch the ground.

He is awfully good – even I can tell that.

I try to look up through the gaps in the chairs, but Dilan prods me. 'Who's that?' he points at the Dad/Granddad man's partner. I examine the pretty teenager swept up in the arms of the youthful Dad/Granddad man. 'I sort of recognise her,' says Dilan. 'She's not Gran, is she?'

'No. Gran died in 1968, when Dad was born, but I recognise her too,' I say, watching her smile at the man, smile at the seated people and dance backwards at speed.

'Mum and Dad aren't here,' says Dilan in the end, halfway through the tango.

'Um,' says Lorna. 'Nor are Bunfight and Coleridge.'

'Coleridge *and* Bunfight? Who is Bunfight?'

'My girl gerbil. They've escaped.' She shakes out her pockets, the blue carrier bag floats to the ground, but there are no gerbils. I look at her and her face creases up. 'They're lost here; someone'll tread on them.'

'You mean there were two – a boy *and* a girl? Together?'

'You're not serious,' says Dilan.

Lorna nods, her eyes brimming over with tears.

I pick up the carrier bag and examine it for gerbils. I know they aren't there, but I check thoroughly inside and out and hand it back to Lorna, who wipes her eyes on it and jams it back in her pocket.

Dilan lets out a long sigh. 'Well, we'd better look for them then.'

We don't find them. In the end we give up all hope of finding either Mum and Dad or the gerbils and head home across the meadows, Lorna jabbering alongside me, telling me long tales of how utterly cute, lovely and darling the gerbils are.

'. . . and there was the time Bunfight got into the cereal packets in the shop – it was so funny – and when she went to sleep in Mum's slippers . . .'

My mind glazes over, and I think about life without Mum and Dad. We've already run out of money, we'll have to start cooking soon and I don't think either of us has a clue. I realise that for the first time I can remember real-life anxiety is larger than imagined anxiety. I am more worried about food than alien invasion.

Whether that's good or bad, I'm not sure.

We reach the house. It looks exactly as we left it, the back door open, the yoghurt pots standing on the side. The telly still booms on in the lounge.

Silently we open the fridge. There are five yoghurts. They look identical. They also look modern, with thin peely plastic lids and pictures of healthy people smiling over sun-ripened fruit. I hand one to Dilan, one to Lorna and we scour them for sell-by dates. '3rd July 2014,' hisses Dilan. Lorna nods. Mine says the same.

'OK,' I whisper. 'Go.'

As I spoon in the first delicious mouthful, I'm vaguely aware of the door from the lounge opening and the shadowy figure of a bearded stranger rubbing his eyes and raising his hand. But I keep spooning the yoghurt, and by the time I reach the bottom of the pot, we're home again.

'That was amazing,' says Lorna, 'even if I have lost Bunfight and Coleridge. This time-travel lark's a breeze.'

But something's bothering me. When we left, the kitchen was a mess. Mugs of cold noodles, a pile of crumbs and the dishwasher running.

Now it's all tidy. In fact it's tidier than I've ever seen it, and there's a blue jacket hanging over the back of one of the kitchen chairs, with Perrymead Nursing Services embroidered over the pocket.

Chapter 14

'Time for your bath, Arnold,' says the strange woman with the tightly curled hair.

'Granddad?' I say, standing in the doorway to the lounge. 'Who's this?'

'Hello, Bugg, dear,' says the woman. 'Have a good day at school?'

She flashes a smile at me and drags Granddad upright.

'If only it hadn't burned down,' mutters Granddad, playing an imaginary piano with his gnarled old fingers.

'Yes, dear – if only. Now lean on me,' says the woman, gripping Granddad's elbow.

He shuffles upright, muttering. A string of dribble escapes from the corner of his mouth. He looks ten years older than he did when we left. I glance at the coffee table. There's a copy of the paper – 2014 – he can't be older, so what's happened?

'Are you all right, Granddad?'

He straightens, turns to me and mumbles, 'The gerbils . . . the ruddy gerbils. They ate the wires. If it hadn't been for the ruddy gerbils, my lovely pier would still be standing – still there . . .'

'Yes, dear,' interrupts the curly-haired woman. 'If only, if only, our lives are full of if onlies. If we could correct all our mistakes, how different it would be.'

'We'll have to go back to that day. The day we went and lost the gerbils.'

'What difference does it make? The pier burned down anyway a few years later.'

'Yes, but look at him now – he's really lost it. He's really . . . old. The gerbils must have brought on the fire earlier, which destroyed his career earlier too. We must go back and find them.'

'You go – I'll stay,' says Dilan. 'I'm interested in exploring this alternative reality.'

'Can I stay?' says Lorna.

'*No!*' I say. 'They're your blasted Gerbils. I need you to catch them. And Dilan, I don't think you should.'

'I promise to do absolutely nothing.' He glances at Lorna. 'And when I say promise, I mean it.'

'You won't talk to anyone, go anywhere . . .'

'. . . pick any buttercups,' interrupts Lorna.

'I definitely won't pick any buttercups,' he replies.

I can see that we've got it wrong the moment we step out of the garden. The fields are gone, no concrete yet, but someone's scoured the top layer from the ground, leaving mud and puddles. That means it's later than 1969, but earlier than 1974. I wonder how old Dave Dando is. 'This is wrong,' I say. 'We'll go back, have another go and take Dilan with us this time, so we're all together and things can't go wrong.'

'Wait,' says Lorna. 'Can we just have a look? I want to see the shop again – in a different time. I might meet my mum.'

'No, you mustn't meet your mum.'

'Why?'

'I don't think it would be good.'

'What would happen?'

'I don't know. You might . . .'

Lorna runs backwards away from me and towards the town. 'D'you know, you sound like my gran – all worries and "don'ts". Live a little – take a chance.' She bounds off ahead along the path, skipping and singing.

'Lorna!' I shout after her, but she doesn't listen.

I follow her through the beginnings of the building site along the footpath that leads to the shop. A middle-aged man's outside, putting out the newspapers. Lorna sucks in her breath, 'That's my granddad, he must have been really young then. I never met him.' Lorna walks over, but I stay on the other side of the road, a bubble of anxiety forming in my throat. I don't like this. I'm sure she's about to break one of the fundamental rules of successful time travel, although thinking about it, we've probably already broken more than one. The gerbils are a pretty enormous time catastrophe all on their own.

Lorna wanders up and down outside the shop, pretending to look at the flip-flops, but actually staring at the bloke.

'Lorna,' I call. 'Come on! We should get going.'

The man looks up. 'Lorna, that's a pretty name.'

I glare at her. She flashes the man a smile. 'Thank you. It is, isn't it?' And she comes back over the road towards me, beaming. 'Let's go and see the pier, see if it really did burn down cos of Bunfight and Coleridge.'

We walk through the streets. They're busier than in 1969, more cars, one or two gardens turned into driveways, advertisements plastered on telegraph poles. It's all shinier, newer, but somehow uglier too.

The pier's gone. The lovely little booths have gone too. A thread of manky barbed wire crosses the entrance, and a few feet of wooden boardwalk end in charcoal. The metal framework scattered with burned fragments of the magnificent ballroom stands in a quiet sea, marking out the full size of the building. It smells of wet fires, and there's no moss on the wood, so it must have happened quite recently.

'Wow,' says Lorna. 'Bunfight and Coleridge did that?'

'Or their grandchildren,' I say.

'Or their great-grandchildren,' says Lorna. 'Or their children's children's children's children. Or their children's children's children's children's children? Or their children's children's children's children's children's children's children. Or their—'

'Thank you,' I interrupt.

'But think how adorable that would have been? Thousands of gerbils racing up and down the curtains.'

I imagine the Castle Ballroom running with rodents.

Just next to the entrance, a man on a ladder is putting

the final coat of paint on a new sign: 'HENDERSON'S CAR SHOWROOM'. Another man pastes big paper notices onto the glass. '*Store opening tonite.*'

'Oh, Henderson's. They're still going. I wonder what the Hendersons themselves looked like then?' Lorna stares in through the window.

Inside, at the back, a teenager and a middle-aged bloke are frantically polishing cars. They're talking and laughing and, because the street's so quiet, I can hear what they're saying.

'What a stroke of luck, Dad,' says the lad.

'Not jokin', son,' says the man, pouring white liquid on the bonnet of the car. 'Been waitin' for something like that to 'appen – didn't even need much 'elp in the end.'

'Miracle,' says the teenager.

'You have to make your own luck, know what I mean? Anyway, we're squeaky clean. No one can touch us. Not our fault, none of it.'

'Sleep easy in your bed, Dad?'

'Exactly, my boy. Someone comes up to you and says, "Young Eddie Henderson, where was you when the fire started?" You can swear on your granny's pillowcase that you was tucked up in front of the telly – cos you was. And you was witnessed there, by the vicar, who happened to call on your mum.'

'Cos I was at home.'

'Cos actually the gerbils did it.

'Yes, it was them that ate the cables that started the fire.'

'Them that chewed through the sprinkler system.'

'Maybe it was even them that made the phone call that

71

took the fire brigade over to the electric factory when the sparks started to fly under the pier.'

'What clever gerbils they must be.'

'And it was nothing to do with me – I wasn't here all the time.' The son laughs, and the man on the ladder coughs.

We're in the way, so we cross the road and head out of town in the direction of the house.

Lorna skips along the pavement, singing to herself. I follow more slowly, trying to make sense of what I've just heard. *Phone call?*

Phone call?

'Bugg. Bugg!' Lorna calls back towards me. 'Race you back to now. Last one back's a loser.'

Slowly I break into a trot and pick my way between the puddles back to our house. I pass Lorna, crash in through the back door, yank open the fridge door and I've already eaten half a yoghurt before she makes it into the room.

'Loser,' I say, as the kitchen morphs into the now.

Chapter 15

Yoghurt gets a little sickly after three pots. But Dilan's standing there, waiting for us, and he immediately hands me another one. 'Wrong year, wasn't it?' he says.

I nod, tearing the lid from the new pot.

'Thought so,' he says. 'I've been comparing pots. And the scary woman's still here. She's making Granddad eat stew and dumplings. It's a horrible scene, gravy carnage, slime, the whole works. Anyway, these should work.'

Before I start on the new yoghurt I fill a sparklingly clean glass from the tap and glug it down. Lorna becomes completely solid alongside me and grabs another glass.

'When we get back,' I say, 'remind me to tell you about Henderson's.'

'Henderson's? Why?' asks Dilan.

'Because,' I say, taking my first spoon of yoghurt and having the fleeting thought that perhaps it's not chance sending us from one year to another, but the fridge. 'For now I need to get back and sort out the gerbils, and then there's Mum and Dad. The other stuff can wait.'

Lorna stands next to me, and fiddles with the letters on

the fridge door. U ACTION, NO I C U AT, CAUTION.

'What other stuff, Bugg?'

He's too late. The kitchen floor fades, and chequered lino takes its place.

Our kitchen in 1969 looks exactly like it did last time. The only difference is that I'm far more worried; we can't live with missing parents and the scary clean woman, or at least not for long.

We arrive at the same time as Dilan and me do the first time, and I shove Lorna out through the door while my previous self is taking in the surroundings.

'What's the rush?' says Lorna, stumbling along the footpath.

'We need to stay out of sight of ourselves and get there before the gerbils get loose.'

'OK,' she says cheerfully. And to be fair, she makes a real effort and runs through the meadow, skipping through the tussocks almost as fast as me although I still don't think she has the faintest idea why.

I glance back. In the distance I can see the other me, Lorna and Dilan arguing about staying or going. It's the weirdest feeling ever.

We run past the woman with the pram and the little girl and the kite. She smiles at us.

'Hello,' I say. 'Lovely day.'

'Yes,' she says. 'Isn't it.'

In a moment we're going to pass her again. I wonder if she'll notice.

When we reach the pier, we don't bother with the man in the booth, just race down the side and up the ladder. The barnacle limpet things look exactly the same, but this time they're not as scary as the idea of not finding the gerbils.

'So are we going to find ourselves in there?' asks Lorna, clambering up the ladder. 'Will we meet ourselves? Should we meet ourselves?'

'Yes, we could meet ourselves, but, no, I don't know if we should. I don't know what really happens if you do, but I don't think it's a good idea.' I step out onto the pier. 'In everything I've ever read, meeting yourself has meant . . .' I hold my hands up to show an empty space. 'Ping!'

'Who pings exactly?' she asks. 'You or the other you?'

I shrug. 'How can you tell which one's which?'

Lorna tilts her head and wrinkles up her nose. 'I'd rather not ping, if you don't mind,' she says.

I don't answer, and push the 'NO ENTRY' door, just like last time. I can't see a thing and have to stand at the back blinking at the glitter ball as the brightest thing in the room.

'We must have been over here when we lost them,' says Lorna, crawling under the seats.

'We were,' I whisper. 'But we're going to have to stay hidden until we see the gerbils escape, and then we'll have to do the best we can to catch them without being spotted.'

'Otherwise, ping,' says Lorna.

I nod.

Three figures come in through the door. I recognise Dilan's silhouette, but not my own. They crawl in under the seats until they're sitting really close to us, so close I can see the hairs on Lorna's legs, and hear myself breathe.

If I reached out my arms I could touch myself. It's almost tempting, but I don't know what would happen and so I won't risk it.

Instead I glue my eyes to the new Lorna's pockets. It takes less than a minute for the first gerbil to make an attempt at escaping. It sticks its nose over the rib of the pocket and clambers out.

It sniffs the air and plunges down towards the floor.

The second one follows.

The real Lorna kneels forward and grabs the first one, handing it to me while she leans to catch the second one.

I hold the little thing close in my hands and pray that it doesn't bite. It's warm and soft and squeaky.

The previous versions of ourselves starts to search for the gerbils. We crawl around from one side of the audience to the other, keeping our heads down and waiting. We really mustn't interfere with anything, otherwise we might get stuck in some kind of time limbo.

Maybe that's what ghosts are – people who time-travelled and got stuck.

I'm just thinking about this when I notice that the other Lorna and Dilan and Bugg have left.

'Whew!' says the real Lorna next to me, and holds up her gerbil to kiss its nose. A nose that's pointy and very like her own. 'Well done, Bunfight. You made it back to Mummy, safe and sound.'

I'm not going to explain to Lorna why she couldn't possibly be mother to a gerbil, but I'm sure I'm still sitting staring open-mouthed at her when the one I'm holding, Coleridge, makes a lunge for it and leaps from my hands.

'Aaaargh!' screams a woman. 'Children!' she shouts. 'There are children under the seats – with rats!'

'Quick, run,' I yelp, diving towards the escaped gerbil, grabbing it with one hand and using the other to slide backwards under the seats before heading for the door.

'Not so quick, nipper,' says a big man blocking the exit, reaching out towards me. 'Let's have a look at your ticket.'

'Bugg!' yells Lorna. 'This way!'

I look back and see her charging straight for the dance floor and the main exit. 'Sorry,' I say, as I duck around the big man, feel his fingers trail across my T-shirt and follow her through the dancing couples. They barely miss a beat, shimmying around us, closing the gap behind, all net, make-up and sequins. The Granddad/Dad man and his partner sidestep to let us through, and she slips me a wink, and for a moment she looks exactly like someone I know, but I can't think who, and I really want to stop and talk to them, but all I can say is, 'Sorry,' before the house lights come up and I realise I'm going to be caught if I don't speed up.

We make it out through the doors and keep running. Before long we're clear of the pier. Lorna dodges through the streets until we're back near the shop, where she stops and sinks to the ground laughing and coughing. 'That was great! Can we do it again? I could smell the make-up.'

I'm breathless, I can hardly speak, but I'm so furious with her I force the words out: 'If you'd left your stupid gerbils at home in the first place, none of this would have happened.' I hand Coleridge over. He's curled into a tiny ball and letting out what I suppose is a gerbil moan. A sort of squeak really.

Lorna snatches him off me and rams him into her cardigan pocket. 'I always have them, except for school. Mum makes me keep them in separate cages. This is the only way they can be together.'

'Well, I wish you didn't, and I wish you'd just do what you said you'd do. You were supposed to be looking after Granddad.'

Lorna sticks her tongue out and opens the side door of the shop. The private door.

'What are you doing?' I say.

'Getting something to eat. I'm interested – do they have Cheesy Crunchers in 1969?'

'You can't.'

'It was my great-grandpa that started the shop. I don't think it would be stealing.'

'But they wouldn't know that. Supposing they caught you? You can't possibly explain.' Surely she couldn't be so stupid.

But she could. I stand out on the pavement as she vanishes inside, feeling ridiculously anxious. What happens if she gets caught? What would happen if we ended up in a police cell? How could we possibly explain ourselves? I imagine 1960s policemen calling in 1960s social workers. Did they even have social workers then? I have completely stopped breathing.

'There!' says Lorna, bursting out of the shop and holding open her blue carrier bag. 'Crisps,' she announces. 'I think.'

I look inside: two blue and white waxy paper bags.

She plunges her arm in, pulls out a packet, rips open the top and tips the crisps into her mouth. They cascade across the pavement. '*Yuck!*' she splutters. 'What's this?' She picks a tiny blue rectangle from out of her mouth.

'Salt,' I say, reading the outside of the other packet. 'You add your own salt.'

'It's disgusting,' she says, dropping the crisp packet back inside the carrier bag and throwing both onto the pavement. 'I need something to drink.' She turns and rushes back into the shop. I carefully tear the top off my salt sachet and shake it into the bag. The crisps are oilier, more delicious than now crisps, and the salt sticks to them in big crunching grains.

Lorna bursts out of the door clutching a large bottle in her arms. 'Run!' she yells, and races off down the street.

I hesitate. '*Hey, stop!* Thief!' A grey-haired man charges out of the shop. 'I'll call the police,' he shouts. 'I've got your description. Nowhere to run to in this town.'

A bubble of panic rises in my throat and my attempt to run away stalls. 'How much?' I squeak. 'How much is the bottle?' I daren't mention the crisps.

The man turns towards me. 'Sixpence – why? Are you offering to pay?'

A gust of wind bowls down the lane, catching the carrier bag that Lorna abandoned, scattering the contents. The grey-haired man manages to get the crisp packet, but the carrier bag fills like a balloon and scuds along the pavement. I try to stamp on it with my foot, but each time I get close it leaps a little and settles further down the street.

'Sorry,' I say, abandoning the bag. I plunge my hand into my pocket and bring up the mix of old and new coins. He steps forward, grips my extended wrist and picks a threepenny piece and three big dirty coppers from my palm. I notice as he does so that at least one of them wasn't minted until 1970, and I hope very much that it doesn't cause some kind of hideous time accident.

Still gripping my wrist, he looks into my eyes. I notice that he has the same mouth as Lorna, slightly too big. 'I'll let you off the crisps. I can see you haven't got enough money. But I'd better tell your parents. Where do you live?'

'Out of town,' I say, waving towards the west as if we might come from miles away. 'But,' I say, pointing at the carrier bag now scudding along the road, 'I should . . .'

The man's face drops. He's giving up.

'I should get the bag.'

'Off you go, but you're both banned from my shop without an adult. Got it?' He lets go and I run after the bag which is now hovering above a post box at the other end of the pavement. I can't see Lorna, which is just as well because if I was to get near her at this moment I think I'd have to kill her, if only to save the world. The bag seems to have its own power source and is getting further and further ahead.

I follow it around a corner, almost reaching it, before a car sweeps by, whisking it high into the air and over the sea wall.

'Yay!' says Lorna, running up alongside me. 'That was hilarious.'

I'd like to throw her over the sea wall, but instead, I say,

'You nearly got us arrested.'

It sounds feeble and she shrugs.

'Lucky I had Granddad's money. Anyway, you shouldn't steal.'

'Honestly, Bugg, it was only two and a half p. I doubt he'd have called the police. Here, try this, it's delicious.'

She hands me a big clear glass bottle with a bobbly texture. 'Cream Soda', it says. I take a gulp. It's like drinking warm vanilla ice cream. I'm not sure it's entirely pleasant, but I'm so thirsty I don't really care. We turn back and walk on past the shop into the countryside, finding the little path we took before. Butterflies flap past, and swifts swoop and dive on us. It's really beautiful, but I'm still completely furious with Lorna. It's as if she has no idea what can happen if you change things.

A fresh yellow butterfly whisks past the end of my nose and lands on a tall yellow plant. It's drying its wings in the sun. Despite my anger, I pause to watch. I can't imagine how anyone drove the first bulldozer into this, destroyed the hedgerow, dug up the grass. It so pretty, so green and alive.

Our little house stands like a white island in the green, tall hedges cuddling around it, keeping it snug.

We walk up to the hedge and peer into the garden. This time there's a man digging a hole. He's got his back to us and he's listening to a little transistor radio on a chair. Distorted rock-and-roll music blares out, covering the sounds of our feet on the gravel driveway. I tiptoe, but Lorna makes a run for the kitchen door. I follow and crash into her back where she stands just inside the doorway, about an inch from a large, aproned woman holding a rolling pin in her left hand and Lorna's arm in her right.

'Who,' she demands, 'are you?'

'Ah,' says Lorna.

I pull open the fridge, grab two modern-looking yoghurts, the spoons we used earlier and rip off the tops.

'I beg your pardon! What on earth are you thinking of? Helping yourself to food from my fridge!'

'I'm really sorry – Mrs –' I say, plunging the spoon deep into the first pot and feeding it to Lorna. 'But we have to –'

'That's what happened last time. That's what that other boy said. Well, I've a mind to call the police. Jack! Jack, we've a pair of young burglars!' she shouts at the open door.

I cram two more spoonfuls into my mouth, and two more into Lorna's – the large woman is starting to fade.

Another spoon, and another, and another, and the kitchen fades, the woman's gone. So's the kitchen.

I look down at my feet.

Shingle.

Chapter 16

'What?' says Lorna, looking around. 'Oh my days! What's happened?'

There's nothing. We're on shingle, but it's not by the sea. The sea's miles out there with the remains of the pier. The pier that actually looks more complete than anywhere else here. The beach seems to have come right inland. All there is in the landscape is a huge bank of stones, some patches of grass, reeds, lumps of rusty concrete, a bin and a sign sticking out of the ground.

No houses, no estate, no nothing.

There's the fridge of course. Standing there, all on its own, no electricity – no chance of electricity, humming. Actually, growling.

'Is this now,' asks Lorna, turning towards me, 'or have we ended up in, like, 2050? You know, after the end of television and stuff.'

I look around for anything that's going to tell us when we are. Inland, sand dunes stretch away towards a line of pylons, and in the distance are storm clouds.

There's nothing of any use at all. I wander over to the sign.

'*Approximate site of the town of Shabbiton. Here, during the heavy rainstorms of the summer of 1969, a small but vital land drain was blocked by litter, undermining the subsoil and destroying the small town. One of the few remaining features of the town is the pier, and at low tide the streets are still visible under the sand. 6,600 people lost their homes.*'

I can't actually speak.

'But that's impossible,' says Lorna, taking one of the gerbils out of her pocket. 'I mean, where's it gone? Where are all the bricks? All the stuff?' She looks around frantically. 'Where's the shop?'

I glance in the direction of the shop. It's not there. Nothing's there.

Nothing's been there for forty-five years. The sea's slowly taken over the land, piling stones and sand on what was left.

She goes over to read the sign again. 'Oh no,' she says eventually. 'It was that carrier bag, wasn't it? I shouldn't have let it go.'

I nod. I'm so cross with her I can hardly think. First her gerbils, then theft and now her litter – does she have no understanding of time and consequence? For a few minutes I pace up and down the shingle, grinding it under my shoes. And then I begin to wonder where my family would be. If they don't live in Shabbiton, where would they have ended up? And if I did find them, do I already exist? How would my parents react to having two Buggs? Would I become twins? Which head would I occupy, or would I flit from one head to the other – or would I actually just melt into myself? I turn back to the fridge. It looks smug, really smug, like it's taught us a lesson. I open the door. It's completely empty, except for two foil-topped yoghurts in glass pots.

'I think,' I say, 'that the fridge is giving us another chance.'

Once again we arrive in the painted kitchen and it's beginning to feel familiar. A millisecond before the kitchen comes into focus I see myself and Lorna, occupying the same space. There is nothing to do but throw ourselves under the table. We watch ourselves leap out through the door, and also watch me and Dilan examine the kitchen. When we've left, we wait for the other Lorna to arrive, examine the kitchen and run out of the back door. I'm terrified that the huge woman will appear, but equally I don't want to rush into any impossible encounters with ourselves. So we watch the clock crawl around to six o'clock before we follow down the path, keeping out of sight and ducking in and out of the hedgerows.

'What are we going to do?' says Lorna. 'What's the plan?'

I look over to her. She's still got the faintest trace of blood under her nose. That was today. In the now. But we've been going back and forth for hours, even though it still looks as if it's six o'clock. I'm starting to get tired, and irritable, and once we've solved the drain thing I AM NOT LETTING HER TIME-TRAVEL AGAIN.

I am quite sure of that.

In fact, I'm not letting her or her stupid gerbils anywhere near me. Ever.

'We,' I say, 'are going to wait for the bag to blow over the sea wall. We are going to be on the beach. We are going to follow it, to the land drain, and you are going to stick your hands into the drain and take it out. Understood?'

Lorna twists her face as if she wants to object, but I refuse to smile, or even meet her eye, so she sighs and shuffles along the track into town. We're back in the fields with the bees and the butterflies, and, if it wasn't for the stupid carrier bag, I'd like nothing better than to lie on the grass and watch beetles climbing flower stalks. The child runs past us, flying a kite, her mother behind, pushing an enormous pram with a huge parasol on the top.

The woman stares. She doesn't smile. 'Haven't I—' she says.

'Evening!' I yell, walking a little faster. 'But . . .' she calls after me.

'Bye,' says Lorna, kicking a clod of sand from her trainers. Sand from an alternative 2014. Sand that couldn't possibly be there. I let my mind wander into the ramifications of the time crimes we've committed in the last hour or so – or the last forty-five years or so.

Instead of following the path through to the shop, we run straight down towards the sea. This way we can't possibly run into ourselves, although other people have obviously spotted us, or one set of us. I can tell from the strange looks we get. We don't catch sight of ourselves, but I have to keep reminding myself that we could. And that I need to watch out for it.

We don't go as far as the pier. Instead we clamber over the sea wall and drop onto a mat of damp hard sand. The concrete wall runs along the top of the beach. Underneath it, a long metal pipe heads out to sea.

'Is that it?' asks Lorna. 'It doesn't seem to have a way in. I'll go down the end and see.' She charges off across the beach, looking for an opening into the pipe.

Actually I haven't a clue where the land drain is, but I'm not going to tell Lorna that. I'm too furious with her, and I suspect that the big metal pipe next to us is sewage, and no matter what happens to Shabbiton, I'm not tangling with it.

Lorna capers back; she's picked up some seaweed and is popping the bubbles.

'Put it down,' I say.

'What – seaweed? How can that affect anything?'

'Just stop. Don't touch.'

'O–K.' A few drops of rain spot onto the rocks of the beach. She stands and looks up at the clouds. I look up too. Forty-four-year-old clouds, gathering into a grey stormy mass over the sea.

'Beautiful, aren't they?' she says to one of the gerbils. It looks unimpressed and crawls back into the darkness of her hand.

I turn away and watch the wall. Any minute now, the bag should come over the top.

One, two, three, four . . .

I assume it will. I assume that we're there somewhere on the other side of the wall losing it, or maybe it'll just pop out of the air. Or maybe we did things differently this time.

Except we couldn't have done.

It has to be coming.

Nineteen, twenty, twenty-one . . .

Or maybe this time someone else got it.

Thirty-two, thirty-three . . .

The blue carrier bag floats high over the wall, as if taking off on a longer, higher flight.

'Oh no, Bugg! It's too high,' says Lorna, galloping sideways along the beach flapping her arms in the air as if the bag might just give up and land on her.

'It doesn't matter, we just have to see where it ends up.' I say, breaking into a trot.

The bag takes a swing to the right and scuttles along the sea wall, threading its way around the rotting wooden seaweed posts poking out of the sand, moving slightly too fast and too erratically for us to catch it. Finally, just as I'm beginning to wonder if we shouldn't go back in time again and stop Lorna actually bringing the wretched bag, it drops, windless, to lie on the sand.

We race towards it, panting over the shingle, arms outstretched, and as we nearly reach it, it whisks straight into the air like a helicopter and swoops over the wall behind.

'*No!*' shouts Lorna, clambering onto a boulder that butts onto the sea wall and attempting to scramble over. 'Come back here!'

I race back towards a set of steps, charge up them and swing out onto the promenade. The bag's lying in the middle of the road, like it's been run over, but I know if I race up to it, it'll just fill with invisible air and skip over the wall again. It's as if it's alive.

I stroll towards it, not exactly looking at it. It rustles over the tarmac, slowly gaining speed before a car trundles past, whipping it into the air again and taking it down a side street. Once again I break into a trot. Whatever happens, I don't want to lose sight of it. The bag jumps and swoops, vanishing under a shiny car. The car's parked right next to the last in a row of cottages, and the front window is open, I can hear voices from inside. I drop down to my knees and crawl towards the front wheel of the car. The ground is dry, so apart from the gravelly bits digging into my knees, it isn't too unpleasant. When I reach the car, I can see that the bag is on the far side, right by a rainwater gully; a little more wind and it might go straight in, but any rain and it would be dragged down instantly. I think about running back and finding a long stick or something, but the bag might just slip down the hole while I was away. Instead, I lie flat on my stomach and drag myself under the car.

'But there's no way they'll ever let you do that by the pier,' says a woman's voice. 'It's for kiddies and ice creams and that, not cars.'

'Of course, love, but we'll never get anywhere if we can't expand. It's hopeless trying to sell all the cars from the garage out here, and those new Minis are . . .' A car passes so that I can't quite hear. 'We need something to do them credit. We could use your sister's place out there in the fields. Or the plot on the seafront. Would make a lovely forecourt.'

I reach my hand towards the plastic bag and close my fingers. It sags in my hand, as if it's finally giving up.

'You'll never get either. Madge wouldn't agree. She loves that house. And the seafront? Not in a month of Sundays. You'd need the luck of the devil to have that happen. More

89

tea, Ed?' says the woman's voice. 'George?'

'Thanks, Mum,' a boy replies.

I shuffle backwards, grazing my elbows on the tarmac. But I'm not really aware of that. I'm thinking about all the things I've heard back here in the past. This is the same father and son talking. The ones that I saw in 1970-something, polishing cars in the shiny new showroom. In that reality, the pier burned down. In this one, where we caught the gerbils, the pier shouldn't burn down. But it did, because Granddad said it did and it's not there in 2014.

So why did it burn down the second time?

'Bugg?' It's Lorna. She's standing there, holding one of her gerbils, looking really worried. 'Did you get it?'

I hold the bag out past the car wheel and her face creases into a smile. 'Oh, what a relief! Mum would have killed me if I'd lost the shop.'

'Lorna, if you'd lost the shop, she'd never have known it existed in the first place. She'd have grown up somewhere else, with another shop.'

'What?'

I sigh. Some people don't understand the very simplest principals of time travel.

Chapter 17

The man is back in the garden, planting the tree which means that the big apron woman will be back in the kitchen, ready to shout at us. We stop at the garden gate.

'Perhaps we should try a different way?' suggests Lorna, stuffing the gerbils deep inside her pockets.

'Like what?' I ask, but I'm too late to have doubts, because Lorna swings in through the gate.

'S'cuse me, any chance of a glass of water?'

The man straightens up, putting his hand on his lower back as if to push the bottom of his spine into place. 'Ask the missus; she's in there.'

'Here?' asks Lorna, eyes wide, her hand on the kitchen door handle.

The man nods and drives his spade into the ground.

Lorna opens the door and smiles sweetly. 'Hello,' she calls. I lurk behind, ready to run, although where I'd run I can't imagine.

'Yes?' Big apron woman fills the doorway.

'Could we please have a glass of water?'

The woman stares hard at Lorna. 'Do I know you? Were

you . . . ?' but she shakes her head, as if dismissing the thought.

I peer past the woman to the clock over the doorway. Seven thirty-five. We're later than we were last time, she's already met us, but looking at her face she's confused, rather than angry. Which of course you would be if you had two children who appeared and broke into your fridge before disappearing into thin air. And it happened more than once. In fact, from what she said before, several times.

'Water?' says Lorna, stepping right into the kitchen, so that I can stand behind her, my back to the fridge.

The fridge purrs. It lets out a long low rumble.

'Oh yes.' The woman turns her back and reaches up into a painted cupboard for two rounded glasses. 'Water.'

Lorna nudges me, but she doesn't need to. I whip round, yank open the door to the fridge and grab two modern-looking yoghurts. There are no spoons, so I pass one put to Lorna and rip back the lid of my own before tipping the contents down my throat. I gaze out of the window towards the pier as the surroundings fade. It's still there as we go, flag fluttering in the breeze, but by the time everything stops changing, like the blue and white lino on the floor, it's gone – it's burned down.

Chapter 18

Our kitchen's a bomb site just as it should be, and there's no nursing-services coat hanging over the back of a chair.

Lorna immediately starts to play with the plastic letters on the fridge. They've bred since we've been away. CAUTION, TIME, DARE and SMNLND.

'You'd almost think they meant something,' she says, this time writing: TIMED SOME CAR LAND TUN IN.

She takes one of the gerbils out of her pocket and kisses it. 'Can you read it, clever Bunfight? You've time-travelled, you know, and we did it, you clever little gerbil! We saved the world.' I can't be bothered to point out that she nearly lost the world with her stupid carrier bag, so I open the lounge door to check on Granddad. He's waltzing with a small table, swinging it gently from side to side, watching more feathered couples whipping around the dance floor at maximum volume. He seems fine. At least, he seems much more normal than he did after the gerbil version of history, but he's a long way from the man we saw dancing on the pier.

'Where's Dilan?' I ask.

Granddad bumps into the telly, ''Aven't a clue.'

'Granddad – how did the pier burn down?'

Granddad's head swings round to face me. 'They never said.' His face clouds over. 'Or did they?' He looks back at the TV and seems to forget me completely.

'Could they tell what caused the fire?'

Dilan comes into the room and drops his skateboard on the floor. 'Why are we asking this?' he says to me.

'Because it wasn't the gerbils. We rescued them before they did any damage, but it still burned down.'

Granddad pulls his forehead into a frown of concentration and gazes at the swirling figures on the screen. There's only the faintest suggestion of the dashing man we saw in the beautiful ballroom. A tiny spark of youth that leaps into his eyes for a millisecond. 'We were supposed to be dancing that night, me and young Doreen. Doreen was your dad's babysitter, you know – lovely girl. We'd practised and practised; we'd worked so hard. We'd been dancing all day every day—'

'So when did it happen?' I ask, wishing I hadn't interrupted, but desperate to know the answers.

'2nd July 1974.'

I feel a sudden jolt of surprise and turn to Dilan. 'That's when . . .'

Dilan nods and makes the motion of zipping his mouth.

'And it was tragic, tragic – ended my career, you know, mine and others . . .'

'Yes, but Granddad, what actually happened?' says Dilan.

'Yes, how did the fire start?' With my fingertips I clear a circle in the sea of tissues and sit down on the carpet.

Granddad stares out of the window, using the sky for inspiration. 'It was seven o'clock.' He rubs the drip from the end of his nose on his dressing-gown sleeve. 'Seven o'clock, or was it quarter past?' Already, I can see the spark is fading. The old shell covering the young man's memories.

'Around seven then?' says Dilan, whirling the wheels on his skateboard.

There's a long silence. 'Seven fifteen, I think. The judges were due to come in and take their places. We had Ted Mildenhall, from the Palace Dance Theatre in London, and Anita Smears – she was a name back then. I was in the green room, polishing my shoes, again.' He gets up and shuffles across the room to his bedroom door; he opens it and slips inside.

'Has he forgotten what he's doing?' whispers Lorna, settling onto the arm of the sofa, almost the only place not covered in tissues.

But Granddad comes back, the same slow pace, the same bent back. This time he's holding a pair of dusty black shoes. He grips his dressing-gown cuff and rubs the sleeve over the dust. Underneath, the cracked black leather shines.

He lets out a long, shuddering sigh. 'These shoes, my lucky shoes.' He sighs again and sits back, staring at the telly, the shoes slipping to the floor.

'And . . . ?' says Dilan. 'What happened next?'

Granddad's brow furrows, he looks at the back of his hand and leans across to take the remote control from the top of the television. He blinks as if he's waking up. 'Have you got anything to eat? I'm starving.'

Chapter 19

'We were there then,' I say. '2nd July 1974 – it must have been for a reason.'

'No, we weren't. We were in 1969,' says Lorna, sticking her finger into a peanut-butter jar and hooking a blob into her mouth. 'Or was it 1970?'

'No, the first time,' I say. 'We were there that very day – and we met Dave Dando. We were there an hour beforehand.'

Dilan nods. 'We did. Dave Dando at six o'clock on 2nd July – and the pier was still there.'

'So your Granddad was still dancing in 1974?' says Lorna. 'Still that smart bloke in the suit?'

'I can't help remembering him on the dance floor in 1969,' says Dilan. 'Whisking Doreen around, looking so . . . so sharp, so happy.'

'I know,' I say. 'And when we went back to catch the gerbils, he was brilliant – not like . . .'

'Sad,' says Lorna, saying the word in my head. We sit in silence, staring at different things in the kitchen, thinking.

'So somehow we went back to one hour before the fire broke out on the very day that the pier burned down. So if we hadn't panicked –' Dilan stares at me – 'we'd have been there when the fire broke out. We might actually have seen what happened ourselves.'

'So who else would know what happened that night?' I ask in the end, trying to reach for the thing in the back of my mind that's bothering me.

'Why are you so worried about it?' says Lorna. 'What happened, happened – it was meant to happen.'

'Yes,' says Dilan, 'she's right. It was meant to happen. Stuff happens all the time; there are giant natural disasters; people have car accidents. They're awful, but they're not really preventable. I mean, if we all rushed around preventing things that happened, we'd be going backwards all the time. In fact we'd barely ever go forwards.'

'I could, for example,' says Lorna, 'not have banged my nose and had a nosebleed the other day. I could go back in time and stop myself.'

'What good would that have done?' asks Dilan

'Um . . .' Lorna's face falls and she wrinkles her nose up at Dilan in fury.

'But was it?' I ask.

'What?' says Dilan.

'Was it really meant to happen?' I say. 'How do we tell the difference between what was meant to happen and what happened because someone else fiddled with it?'

'You've lost me there, Bugg,' says Dilan.

I try to disentangle all the snippets I've overheard so that I can explain what's been lurking in my head. *That's what that other boy said. Make your own luck. It was nothing to do with me. I wasn't here all the time.* Wasn't here?

'Supposing . . . we weren't the first people to time-travel here, using the yoghurt and the fridge?'

'Is there someone else doing it? Someone in our kitchen we haven't noticed?' asks Dilan.

'Ooh!' says Lorna, looking around for an invisible person. 'I hadn't thought of that. This house was empty for ages before you moved into it.'

'Was it?' I ask.

'Oh yes. Mum said it was a shame, such a lovely house with a lovely garden.'

'Anyway, yes – and no. I don't know exactly if there's anyone else, or who they might be – or at least I'm not sure. It's just I can't help feeling that time's been messed with already. Before we messed about with it.'

Dilan sighs. Lorna fiddles with the fridge letters. I TIMED SCONE AN LARD TUMN.

I stare at the fridge. It howls and tweets, but gives me nothing more.

They all wait for me to explain myself.

'OK, what I mean is, if you watch any film or TV programme about time travel, they always say you mustn't fiddle with time. You could change history, and not always in a good way. You could end up not being born, your parents might not be born – all that stuff. Yes?'

'It's not just films, Bugg, it's you,' says Lorna, sitting back down and flicking a bread crumb across the table. 'Remember all that "ping" stuff?'

'But – supposing someone's changed history already.

Someone's fiddled about with time, messed it up, changed other people's fortunes, bettered their own.'

'You said that,' says Lorna. 'That there's been someone else doing it.'

Dilan looks up. 'Are you saying that we could break the time rules, that we could interfere, because we'd be putting right someone else's time mistakes?'

'Well, yes. Exactly.' I stand up and fiddle with the letters on the fridge. TEND A COLD TRAIN IN SUMMER – I need another R. 'Do you remember what that big woman with the apron said? The one that lived here. Something about what happened last time and a boy.'

'Where's here?'

I point at the floor. 'This house. When Lorna and I went back to 1969 the second time, we met this woman, here in the kitchen. She said something about someone else stealing things out of her fridge.'

'Who – why?' asks Dilan.

'That's why I wanted to ask Granddad about what exactly happened when the pier burned down. The second time – or the real time, the time that we knew about back then, when we were in the now. I want to know who was there and who wasn't. How exactly the fire started and why the fire brigade didn't get there to put it out . . .' I stop. They're both staring at me as if I'm utterly mad. 'And I want to know who lived in this house.'

Dilan leans back in his chair, balancing it on the two back legs. He looks at me sideways. 'Bugg, you are nuts. You do know that? I've spent my whole life proving to you there are no Frankenstein's monsters in the airing cupboard – so instead you've invented a conspiracy theory about a pier, a fridge and a house.'

I think back to the fragments I heard. 'No, it's not a theory. This is definitely real. I can't prove anything because I didn't record anyone saying it, but I'm sure something's going on – not here, not now, but in a parallel time stream, someone's up to no good. Someone from the nearer past visited the further past, and changed history. They did it using this house, this fridge and these yoghurts.'

'Hey.' The door from the lounge swings open and Granddad shuffles in. 'I'm hungry. Any pie or anything?'

I open the fridge. The whole of yesterday's shop is still there, carrots and potatoes and raw meat. Dilan stares in too.

'Not a clue what to do with it,' he says.

I shake my head. I don't know either.

'So are Mum and Dad part of all this, or is that just an accident?' Dilan pokes at a piece of chicken as if it might magically transform itself into a casserole with accompaning vegetables.

'I think Mum and Dad disappearing is an accident,' I say. 'Unless looking for them is part of the whole thing.'

'Hmm,' says Dilan. 'Accident or no, we're going to have to think of a way of getting them back. Just now though, I really wish we could come up with a way of feeding ourselves.'

'I can boil an egg,' says Lorna. 'Would that do?'

Granddad looks at her with appreciation. 'With soldiers?'

Chapter 20

I learn from Lorna how to boil an egg, while Dilan has another go with Granddad. They sit at the kitchen table. Granddad draws pictures in spilled sugar on the top. He draws a pair of high-heeled shoes, with bows.

'So, Granddad,' says Dilan, 'when the pier burned down . . .'

'. . . That was a terrible night. I was polishing my shoes, you know, getting up a shine – shall I show you? I've still got them . . .'

'That's all right, thanks, Granddad. I've seen them. I wanted to know what happened next.'

The eggs come to the boil and Lorna sets a timer.

'As easy as that?' I ask.

She nods. 'Frying them's pretty simple too. Can you make toast?'

'What happened next . . . ?' Granddad stares into the sugar crystals. 'What happened next? I was young once. I'm still eighteen inside, you know. Under this old body. You can't see the young man, can you? Just the old fool.'

None of us quite knows what to say to that.

After a long time I say, 'So, Granddad, can you remember what you did next, after shining your shoes?'

Granddad seems to wake up. He stands, and takes Lorna's hand. 'You don't mind, do you?' he asks. Then, putting his arm gently on her waist and taking a graceful hold of her left hand, he takes half a dozen tiny light steps. For a moment he looks like the Dad/Granddad man we saw back in 1969. Then he swings Lorna round the kitchen table and then releases her so that she spins over to thump against the bin. 'We were going to start with a tango. That was certainly the plan. The ballroom was full, packed to the gunnels. We had Ted Mildenhall judging, you know, and the prize pot was massive.' He picks a noodle from his pyjamas. 'Derek Simmons and Verity Cowley were our main rivals, and they were simmering, dancing out of their shoes that season, but Doreen and I, we had hopes, great hopes.' Granddad slumps back into the chair as if someone's pulled the plug.

The toaster ticks as we wait to hear more, but Granddad's stopped. Like an old record when it runs out and the arm lifts back over to the side.

'So did Derek Simmons and Verity Cowley dance?' I ask in the end.

'What?' says Granddad. 'When?'

'On the night the ballroom burned down,' says Lorna.

'Oh – I can't remember – I just remember the flames. Twice the height of the building they were. Six fire engines, a sea full of water, but they couldn't put it out. They came too late, you see.' He shakes his head. 'Tragic, utterly tragic.' Granddad chops the top from his first boiled egg and the deep yellow yolk pours down the shell. 'It was almost as if it was on purpose.'

I spread butter on the toast and cut it into fingers. Dilan sneaks a slice from the plate, and Lorna looks longingly at the rest of the badly sliced loaf standing on the side.

Almost as if it was on purpose.

Once we've got Granddad settled in front of the TV, and some more eggs on the go, we talk. It feels as if I've been awake for days, which I suppose I have, and I'm starting to get confused.

'So you mean we go back to the day before yesterday to stop the fire? How would that help?'

'No,' says Lorna, stuffing even more bread into the toaster, 'you go back to the now to stop your parents going to the then. And, you go back to the *then* to stop the fire.'

'Both?' asks Dilan.

'I see what you mean,' I say. 'If we could take a yoghurt pot to yesterday – any time yesterday – we could stop them eating the yoghurt.'

'So which one do we do first?' asks Dilan, stuffing in another mouthful of boiled egg.

'The fridge will decide,' I say.

'Huh?' asks Dilan. 'Are you serious?'

'Completely. When we went back to the flooded now, there were only two yoghurts in the fridge. We had no choice. I bet the fridge has already decided what we should do next.'

'Let's see, shall we?' says Lorna. She opens the fridge door. There are no yoghurts.

For one awful moment I wonder if the fridge has stopped working, or decided not to trust us anymore, and then, at the very back, stuck between the mayonnaise and a red pepper, I find two yoghurts, huddled and alone.

I pull them out and examine the labels. '1st July 2014!'

'But what about the fire and changing history?' asks Dilan, looking confused.

'It obviously doesn't think we should do that – yet,' I say, trying to sound as if I believe what I'm saying.

'Right then,' says Dilan, wiping his mouth with the back of his hand. 'Yesterday – or the day before – it is then.' He looks at me. 'Ready?'

'Can I come?' says Lorna.

'No,' we say in chorus, 'you can't'

'There are only two yoghurts,' says Dilan.

'Go home,' I say. 'And we'll see you tomorrow, today, yesterday – whenever it is.'

'Ohhh,' says Lorna, her lip jutting out. 'Unfair.'

'Go on,' I say. 'Or you'll get stuck with Granddad for all eternity.'

'What?' Lorna's eyes widen. 'Surely not.'

I shrug. 'I don't know for certain – but are you prepared to risk it?'

Lorna wrenches open the back door and we see her run across the garden, dive into the maze of streets that make up the estate and vanish.

'Right then, yesterday it is,' says Dilan, brandishing a spoon and plunging it deep into the yoghurt pot.

Chapter 21

It must be the day before yesterday. It's six o'clock, as it always is. Mum's on the phone to her sister; Dad's in the garden; the telly's on next door.

'Is this today? Or yesterday?' asks Dilan.

'The day before that, I think.'

'Shouldn't we jump forward?' he says.

I shake my head. 'We can't be sure we'd get back to the right time. We might miss them. I have a feeling the fridge wants us to try to stay hidden until we reach the point where they disappear.'

Dilan looks worried. 'How do I avoid myself? What would I have been doing?'

'Skateboard?'

'So where shall I hide?'

'Upstairs? Airing cupboard?'

He nods and shuffles upstairs. Outside I hear the other Dilan scrape the wheels of a skateboard on the tarmac.

What was I doing?

I try to think back. I wasn't hanging out with friends – I don't really bother with them. Reading? No, I don't think so. I only read in bed, to stop myself being scared of the things underneath it. So what was I doing? I sit under the table and examine the backs of my hands. There are hairs. Maybe I'm turning into a werewolf. I shake my head; I'm not turning into a werewolf. I've already been to the future. I'm not a werewolf there, so I can't possibly be one here.

At that moment I realise what I was doing the day before yesterday, because I'm doing it again now. Nothing. Nothing at all, just worrying about things. That's how I fill my time. I'm both reassured and disappointed. Do I really fill hours and hours with stupid worries? Is that really what I was doing the day before yesterday?

I really can't think of anything else. I don't watch TV because of Granddad. He's in front of it most of the time, and anyway, Mum says I shouldn't watch anything too grown-up, or anything sci-fi or anything really because all I do is agonise all night about aliens climbing the stairs. I actually don't think what I watch makes any difference. It's being the youngest – it's a lonely place. I'd always be the first one any marauding creature would choose to pick off, the least likely to be able to defend myself.

I sit and imagine life with a younger brother or sister. Would it be better or worse? Less Mum and Dad to go round, more people to talk to. I might start to worry about them. I might feel I had to protect them.

'Bugg, do you want to come for a walk?' It's Mum.

I'm about to answer that I don't want to when I hear myself say, 'No, thanks, Mum.'

I sit under the table until Mum goes and other Bugg goes,

and then run upstairs to join Dilan in the airing cupboard.

Sleeping's weird. Apart from anything else, the airing cupboard is small, and Dilan snores. I don't know if I sleep, or just go into a form of paralysis. I'm paralysed by the idea that the fridge is actually a real being that's trying to control us. After all, it decides when and where we go, by only offering a tiny choice of yoghurts.

I don't think I want to be controlled by a fridge.

I'm also wondering quite how we're going to get through the whole of tomorrow without being spotted. We can't actually spend all day at home. Someone's bound to find us, but then I can't see how we're going to get out either.

In the morning, I hear Mum kissing me and sending me off to school.

'Here's your packed lunch,' she says, stuffing a sandwich bag at the other me. 'And don't forget to walk to the end of the road after school. I'll be able to give you a lift home.'

I gaze at her through the keyhole. I don't think I've ever noticed how nice and kind Mum's face is, sort of squashy and warm. I'd like to give her a hug, but the other me just ducks away from her kiss and runs down the stairs. Mum opens the airing-cupboard door and we shrink into the darkness while she fiddles with a towel before shutting the door again.

I wish I'd thought about this a bit more. Stuck in here, all I can think about is all the fantastic things I could be telling people at school. I could tell them that there will be beef stew on the menu.

I could tell them that Mr Priest, our teacher, will be ill, so we'll have the supply teacher with the big ears.

I could tell them that Dilan will go flying as he steps in through the school gates, that Becky Wen's lunch box will empty across the bus, that Jordan Keating will be sick over Mr Symes, that Mr Todd will be lurking behind the wall ready to bark at anyone with the wrong shoes.

I could tell them all these fantastic things that only someone who has visited the future could know, but no one would ever believe me. They think I'm weird enough as it is. They'd put it down to coincidence and lucky guesses.

And they'd be more interested in why there were two of me.

'I'm hungry,' says Dilan eventually. 'We need to get out of here.' He pushes open the door and pauses on the landing.

'We can't eat anything,' I say. 'It'll affect time.'

Dilan glares at me, slips down the stairs and stops outside the kitchen to listen. Granddad's telly covers the noise of our footsteps, but I can still hear Mum whistling in the kitchen.

'We'll have to go out,' I say, tiptoeing in the direction of the front door.

With a longing look towards the kitchen, Dilan follows and we run into the lane until we're well out of sight.

We spend hours sitting in the churchyard feeling hungry and not touching anything.

We're still wearing our school uniforms, which means that if we get spotted, someone will ask questions. But possibly not as many questions as they would if we weren't.

'I've had enough,' says Dilan. 'If I don't eat something, I'll die.'

'Have you got any money?' I ask, deciding that the least dreadful thing to do would be to buy something, although if we buy something, that's going to mean that someone else doesn't buy it, or that it doesn't get thrown away, can't rot on a rubbish heap, can't feed some beetles that might possibly feed a bird, that might not be caught by a cat that might belong to someone that couldn't afford to keep it, which would mean that the cat would die, and the person would be sad – and then Dilan says:

'No.'

'So where are you going to get food?'

'From school.'

'School? But *we're* at school.'

'Yes – but we know where we are, so we can avoid ourselves.'

'Dilan, you're mad,' I say.

'I'm not; you'll see.'

I argue with him the whole way, but soon we arrive at the gates and let ourselves in. It's lunchtime, and I know that all through lunch that day I was sitting in the classroom worrying about the edge of the universe. If it has an edge, what's beyond it? We'd been doing the cosmos, and the cosmos always makes me feel anxious – it's just so big.

'Hello, Bugg, dear,' says Miss Golightly, catching me sneaking a sandwich from the dining room. 'How's Arnold?'

She wriggles her tongue around her teeth as if to clear the last shards of peanut brittle from her mouth. This time

I notice her smile, her perfect lipstick, the graceful way she lays her hand against her throat.

She's the girl from 1969. I'm sure of it.

So I ask her. 'Miss Golightly, when the pier burned down – what exactly happened?'

A tiny frown crosses Miss Golightly's eyebrows. The corner of her mouth flicks down and then back up into her warm smile. She glances at her watch. 'Goodness, that's a long way back. 1974. Before I started here.' She addresses the playground. 'I was his partner, of course, Arnold, your Granddad.' She swivels to face me. 'Did you know that?'

'Yes – no – I don't know,' I say.

'It was the evening that it happened. We were getting ready to dance. The girls' dressing room was a cloud of hairspray and talcum powder.' Like Granddad, I can see that she's replaying the whole thing.

'And?'

'The first couple would have gone out to dance, and I don't think we knew anything was wrong until we smelled the smoke. The fire alarms didn't work – I don't think they'd been serviced – and the sprinkler system only came on in the foyer. Shirley Sunshine – oh, she wasn't really called that. She was Janet Nobbs. Still is, I expect – she ran in and shouted, "Fire!" We ran. The audience ran too; it was pandemonium.' Miss Golightly lets out a sigh and wipes a tiny tear from her powdered cheek. 'There were an awful lot of people in there that night. It took the firemen an age to arrive, and when they did they had to get us all out before they could even start to put the fire out. It's a miracle no one was killed.'

'Do you remember seeing anyone who shouldn't have been there?' I ask, just as the bell rings for the end of lunch.

'No – well, not really.' She stares into space, remembering. 'There were so many people that night, the promenade was heaving.' She taps me on the arm. 'Run, or you'll be late.'

Chapter 22

Getting into our school was quite easy; getting out is not. We're just swinging through the gate when Mr Todd spots us.

'Dilan, Bugg – into class now.'

'But, Sir,' says Dilan, 'we've got a dentist appointment. It's really important.'

'It is,' I say, putting on my most anxious face.

Mr Todd falters.

Mr Todd is like the school Rottweiler: he never falters.

He checks his watch and scratches his chest. 'It's only one thirty. You'll come back afterwards.'

'We'll come back,' I say. 'You'll hardly notice we've gone.'

Mr Todd obviously doesn't believe me, but he opens the gate and waves us away and we run from the school as hard as we can.

'Now what?' asks Dilan when we've meandered home. 'It's only four o'clock. What are we going to do all evening? I'm not sure I can stand any longer in the airing cupboard.'

He's right; there's hours to go and at the moment we're

hiding in the garden hedge, which is fine, but limiting in terms of entertainment. I spent nearly an hour watching a butterfly laying eggs on Dad's newly planted cabbage plants.

'We could try the shed.'

But the shed's full of Dad's cycling gear and we don't fit, so we go back to the hedge and crouch in the privet studying the game options on Dilan's phone.

At about four thirty Mum's car screeches into the driveway and we watch ourselves rush into the house. At four forty Mum goes back out with a huge pile of shopping bags, and the other Dilan comes out with his skateboard and messes about in the road.

Dilan watches himself, wincing at his own technique. He even has to cover his face with his hands at one point.

Finally Mum comes back with the shopping and crashes in through the kitchen door with the first carrier bags.

I catch a glimpse of myself standing by the fridge.

'We're about to try the yoghurts.' I say.

'Ooh, let's have a look,' says Dilan, leaning towards me and nearly tipping us both out of the hedge.

'Hey,' I shout at him, and I'm sure I see myself look up, just as I see myself fade out of the kitchen.

'How long have we got?' says Dilan.

'I don't know,' I say. 'Seconds, I should imagine.'

We charge through the kitchen. I can't help taking a look at the fridge as we go past and I notice that the one thing that hasn't gone back to yesterday are the letters on the door.

They're in a jumble, except for the word TIME.

'Time,' I say. 'It says time.'

'What says time?' hisses Dilan, diving into the airing cupboard.

'The fridge. I mean, I think it's got a soul. It's an entity – it can think – it can leave messages in the letters.'

Dilan widens his eyes and shakes his head, squeezing himself into the space at the back of the airing cupboard. 'It's just a fridge, with magic yoghurt in it. You know, happens all the time. I expect Mum made the word.'

I shut up and worry while Dilan sends himself texts.

Chapter 23

Hours later, we hear ourselves go to bed. There are lots of tap noises and flushing noises, and giggling on the landing.

The smell of stew drifts up the stairs. 'I'm really hungry,' says Dilan.

'So am I,' I say, thinking about Dad's stew.

There are clanking noises in the kitchen, shuffling from Granddad, and then he turns the telly up really loud so that we can hear the laughter from the dance show that he's watching.

'Now what?' hisses Dilan.

'We wait for Mum to come back.'

'Uh? We won't have time to stop them.'

'Her dirty plate was on the side – she must have eaten supper before the yoghurt.'

The car scrunches over the gravel in the drive. The door slams, and Mum's key rattles in the lock.

'Now?' asks Dilan.

'Yes – now.'

'Stop!' hisses Dilan. 'We're still in school uniform. They'll know something's up.'

We rummage in the shelves above our heads for pyjamas. I have to wear a pair of Mum's pyjama bottoms and I just hope she doesn't notice. Dilan opts for pants.

We crawl to the top of the stairs. It's hard to make out what's going on because of Granddad's music which I can feel through my toes.

'Go on,' says Dilan. 'Or we'll miss them.'

I take a deep breath, straighten up and tiptoe down the steps. From the hall I can see into the kitchen, and Mum and Dad are sitting on either side of the table. They've got a glass of wine each, and two unopened yoghurts sitting on the table between them.

Behind them, the fridge is humming. Mum reaches out for one of the pots.

'No!' I say.

But Mum's peeling off the lid.

'No! Don't eat it!' I yell, staggering forward, clutching my stomach with one hand, my mouth with the other. 'There's something . . .' I rush to the sink and make exaggerated vomiting sounds, turning the tap on with such force it soaks my pyjama top but blending my pretend, invisible vomit into a mix of washing-up residue. 'Aaaaaaarghghghghgh.'

'Bugg!' Mum throws the yoghurt to one side. 'You poor darling. Dilan, quick, get a towel!'

Dilan appears in the kitchen doorway, trying really hard not to laugh. 'Sure,' he mutters, and belts up the stairs.

I sink theatrically to a chair and groan while Mum stands behind me, stroking my shoulders. Dad peers in the sink and frowns. 'Not much came up then?' he says.

'It was all milky – it's the yoghurt,' I say, slipping one of Granddad's packet soups under my top and running for the downstairs loo. I chuck it down the loo, which smells of Granddad's wee, and nearly vomit for real. After flushing, only the squares of carrot float to the surface. It looks quite convincing. 'Ugh!' Sagging to the floor in the hall, I stuff the empty packet into the pyjama bottoms so that Mum can't see it and roll from side to side.

'Mum – who lived here before us?' I ask.

'What a funny question when you're in the middle of being sick,' says Dad. 'Old Margaret, she'd lived here for years – since the Fifties, I think – all my life anyway.'

'Did you ever come in the house, Dad?'

'Oh, do stop talking about that now. Bedtime,' says Mum, 'with a bucket, and no school for you tomorrow.'

'Oh!' I say, wondering how I'm going to explain this to the sleeping Bugg. 'Really?'

'Really.'

Chapter 24

'But I wasn't sick,' says the other Bugg.

'Don't be silly,' says Mum. 'That's why you changed your PJs. Dad's going to stay home to look after you.'

'What?' squeals the other Bugg.

The other Dilan, and the Dilan with me inside the airing cupboard, laugh.

'You'll be fine – and I've thrown away all the yoghurts, although there seemed to be an awful lot of them. Far more than I remember.'

'Really?' asks the other Bugg anxiously.

'Oh yes,' says Mum. 'I keep on finding more and more – most mysterious. Anyway, I'm off to work.'

'More and more yoghurts? What's the fridge playing at?' I say to Dilan. 'We need to take a look.'

'Shh,' says Dilan. 'She's going out. Won't the other Bugg take a look?'

'Exactly. We need to get there first, in case the other Bugg decides to take another trip.'

'Will the other Bugg take another yoghurt trip? Won't the other Bugg be too scared without me alongside?'

I can't see whether Dilan's smiling, but I suspect he is.

'Can't chance it. I need to go down.'

Mum's car engine starts up outside. I creep out of the airing cupboard and slope down the stairs into the kitchen. Granddad's standing there, playing with the letters on the fridge.

'Look,' he says. 'My name. ARNOLD.' He fiddles around with the remaining letters.

'Can I just have a look in the fridge, Granddad?' I say.

He nods, his face pulled into deep thought, and moves to one side. He goes on playing with the letters as I look inside. Six more yoghurts.

'Stop,' I say. 'Stop, fridge.' I pull out the tubs and drop them in the bin.

'What?' says Granddad.

'Nothing, Granddad,' I say. But something occurs to me and I lean forward and whisper to the fridge. 'I know, fridge. I know that if Mum and Dad don't go back in time, or forward or wherever it is they go, we won't go and look for them. If we don't go and look for them, then we won't see what we saw, we won't hear what we heard. We won't know that the pier didn't burn down on its own. But it's all right, because we've heard and seen it not; it can't be taken away from us – we don't need to go and look for Mum and Dad.'

'And, DANCE,' Granddad announces. 'ARNOLD MUST DANCE IN TIME,' he announces.

Behind me the door opens. There's nothing for it – I have

to dive into the pile of dirty laundry.

Dad's feet sound on the kitchen floor.

'Arnold must dance in time,' says Granddad carefully. 'Did you hear that?'

Dad sighs. 'If only.'

I'm squashed in next to Dilan's dirty socks for ages, so long that my leg goes to sleep and I can't actually work out where it is. While I'm there, I think all this time stuff through again.

It occurs to me that the other Bugg must go to school. If Bugg misses school, then Lorna won't come back. She might still do the trust game and get a nosebleed, but Miss Golightly will go back to Lorna's house and won't come here.

Would that matter?

It would because of the gerbils and the plastic bag.

Without the whole gerbil thing, I wouldn't have overheard the conversations, and we wouldn't know that someone else had time-travelled. But on the other hand, the fridge now knows that we know, so it might not feel like it has to send us back to do the gerbil thing.

I think.

There's also the small matter of all these simultaneous timelines. If there are two Buggs and two Dilans wandering around, won't there be two Buggs and two Dilans forever? But then the person who interfered with time before us would also be wandering around in multiple forms and I can't think that they'd have managed to keep it going for forty-five years. There must be a moment, like the real present, when the timelines join up. When Bugg One and

Bugg Two become a single Bugg.

I hope.

Eventually I creep back up and sit with Dilan in the airing cupboard. He's been to his room and brought his entire stash of uneaten Christmas chocolate. It's white and fuzzy in places, but I'm not going to turn it down.

'How worried are you then?' he says. 'On a scale of one to ten.'

'I think,' I say, 'that we need to get back to now – to tomorrow. I think if we don't something very confusing will happen with Lorna and there will be too many of us trying to sort this out.'

Dilan sucks on a white chocolate reindeer. It might never have been white; it might only be white now.

He nods. 'OK,' he says. 'I think you're right – and to be honest, I'm getting pretty bored in here.'

I change back into my school uniform. We sneak down the stairs, and open the fridge door. Two yoghurts. New-looking ones, and the date is 3rd July 2014.

'That's today – isn't it?' says Dilan.

'Yes – but later on. It's always six o'clock.'

He nods wisely and rips the top off one of the yoghurt pots, but I know he doesn't really understand.

The tidy world we're in fades and reappears, but this time with Lorna in it.

'Wow – how did you get here?' says Dilan.

'I've been here almost the whole time. You've only been gone a few minutes – but you'll be glad to know that I took my gerbils home,' she announces. 'And I haven't got any carrier bags or large pieces of plastic, or anything really. Oh, and I asked my mum about the house.'

'And?' asks Dilan.

'Margaret, otherwise known as old Madge, used to live here.'

'Madge?' I say, trying to remember where I've heard the name.

'Margaret, sister of Charlotte,' says Lorna deliberately. 'Charlotte *Henderson* – married to George.'

'Eddie Henderson's aunt?'

'Hang on – what's that got to do with anything?' says Dilan.

'Everything, and maybe nothing,' I say. 'So Eddie would have had access to the house?'

Lorna nods. 'Yes – he would. Mum said that when Madge got really old, Eddie would come and go with her shopping. She said he was really quite kind. Most unlike him.'

'Tell me, is there another Bugg out here somewhere?'

'What?' Lorna says. 'No – just you.'

'But did you do the whole falling over thing with the nosebleed?'

'Yes. And your mum picked us up from school, like she said she would, and now she's gone out.'

'Really?'

'Yes, you were late, but . . .' She shrugs.

Dilan smiles at me. 'That. Is. Awesome.' He opens the

fridge. There are three yoghurt pots, old ones with the foil lids.

'Are there only three?' I ask, examining the pot for a sell-by date.

'Only three, so these have to be the ones,' he says, pulling out three spoons.

'Ready?' I ask, and plunge my spoon deep into the pot, savouring every delicious mouthful and remembering the instructions from the fridge.

'Gordon Bennett! What you wearin'?' says Dave Dando, twirling his bike. He's pointing at Lorna's school trousers.

'School uniform,' says Lorna, staring down at her legs. 'What sort of bike is that?'

'You know – a Chopper – five-speed, see?' The boy fiddles with a large black ball on the end of a chrome stick. He weaves out across the play park and back, the front wheel wobbling from side to side. 'Anyway, you look ridiculous,' he says. 'Surprised your mum let you out like that.' He stops, climbs off his bike.

Lorna raises an eyebrow at Dave's jeans

'Weren't you here a minute ago?' he says.

'Yes,' I say.

'No,' says Dilan.

'But without her?' says Dave Dando.

'Did you say your dad was a fireman?' I say casually.

Dave stares at me. 'Yes, about fifteen seconds ago,' he says. 'When you walked out of the playground that way.' He points towards the town. 'How did you do that? How did you get back round?'

'Um,' I say.

Lorna giggles and we all glare at her.

'Anyway – better get going,' I say. 'Bye for now.' But Dave accompanies us across the playground, pulling wheelies behind us.

'What time is it?' mutters Lorna.

'Must be around six. It always is,' I say.

'We've got an hour until the fire,' says Dilan.

'No,' I correct him. 'We've got an hour to stop the fire.'

Everything is very much exactly the same as our first visit to 1974. Except that Dave Dando follows us.

'How did you do that so quickly? How did you get round?'

'We're quick,' I say hopelessly.

He lurks on his Chopper as we pass the shop. Lorna checks the date on the newspapers. '2nd July 1974.'

'Of course,' says Dave. 'Why wouldn't it be?'

Chapter 25

Crowds of people mill around the entrance to the pier.

'Dance competition,' says Dave. 'No fun at all – all that flouncy stuff.'

'Well,' says Lorna, reaching into her pocket and pulling out a handful of change. 'This time we should be able to pay.'

'You goin' in?' asks Dave, his jaw dropping. 'Boys don't go to things like that.'

I rather wish Dave would disappear. I don't want to explain everything to him, but then, I don't want a scene either. 'Do you want to come too? We might have enough money.'

'If you're payin'.' Dave props his bike against the railings and stands in the queue with us. 'So long as no one from school sees me.' He fiddles with the zip on his jacket and stares at Dilan's shorts as if he's not sure if he should be doing this.

I help Lorna count out four pounds. All the coins are bigger, and we don't quite have enough. I fumble in my pocket and find another of Granddad's old coins, an old fifty-pence piece. We give the money to the man in the booth, who raises his eyebrows and hands us four small white tickets.

We show them to a woman dressed from head to toe in turquoise. She's talking to another woman, and barely notices us. 'Oh yes, Ted Mildenhall, I believe, and apparently he's a big fan of Arnold's.'

'Ooooh – how thrilling,' says the other woman, and she pats the back of her rock-hard hairdo as if it might have collapsed.

The ballroom is extra sparkly, and extra busy. Even the women in the audience are wearing feathers and sequins, and all the men have suits. We must look really peculiar, especially Dilan in his shorts. No one in 1974 has ever seen a pants-waistband sticking out over the top of someone's trousers before – it's obvious that they haven't, and people stare and point.

'Should we sit down in the audience?' whispers Dilan.

'We've paid, we're entitled to a seat,' says Dave, squeezing onto the end of a row, next to an enormous man, and crossing his arms.

'I think we need to take a look around,' I say. 'And I think you should pull your T-shirt down over the top of your shorts.'

Lorna hides a smirk as Dilan yanks up his shorts and drags down his T-shirt, trying to hide the pants gap.

Leaving Dave in the ballroom, we trail back out into the foyer. I'm looking for Eddie Henderson, the young version, but I can't see him anywhere. Perhaps I'm completely wrong about this. Perhaps he's got nothing to do with the pier, with time travel, with any of it.

While I'm combing the crowd, Lorna marches up to a door marked DRESSING ROOMS and pushes on through. Dilan follows and I hesitate outside, feeling foolish, trying to look as if I'm reading a poster but actually checking everyone as they enter.

A moment later, and the dressing room door bursts open, releasing a cloud of suffocating hairspray. Dilan and Lorna stumble into the foyer propelled by the man who threw us out the first time we came here. 'Out! No kids in the dressing rooms. It's a serious competition, you know. We can't have you lot mucking about back here.'

Lorna sticks out her tongue as the man vanishes behind the door. Dilan pulls up his shorts and sweeps his hair back. 'Well,' he says, 'I don't think anyone could get past him.'

'Dilan's right,' says Lorna. 'The security's very tight.'

I gaze at the closed door. 'If that's the case, then the fire must have started outside.'

'But there isn't an outside,' says Lorna.

'Let's look,' I say, and we shuffle past the turquoise woman.

'You can't just wander in and out, you know,' she says.

'I need to check on my bike,' says Lorna.

'Yes,' says Dilan. 'We're checking with her, aren't we, Bugg?'

'Yes,' I say. 'We're all checking. On the bike.'

The woman frowns at us, but what must be a coach party arrives with lots of noise and women rushing for the cloakroom, and the foyer fills up, giving us the chance to run outside. Clutching the tickets, I stand on the road and look back at the pier. Lorna's right – there isn't really an outside on the sides, just a narrow strip of wood and lots of ironwork. For a moment we stand and watch the whole area.

'I can't see anyone doing anything,' says Dilan.

'No,' says Lorna. 'But in just over half an hour the whole thing is going to burst into flames.'

'We can't stop it before it starts if we don't know where it starts,' I say.

The other two look doleful. Dilan hitches up his shorts for the millionth time, and Lorna fumbles in her empty, gerbil-free pockets.

I think of Dave sitting inside, waiting for the action to start. 'On the other hand,' I say, 'we could call the emergency services here, so that they're already on the scene when the fire starts.'

'But they might not make the fire happen if the emergency services are here,' says Lorna.

'They're time-travelling. They have to come back to now. The fridge must have sent them to now. Their piece of time travel has already happened.'

'Hang on,' says Lorna. 'You mean that whoever started the fire was sent back by the fridge? But why is the fridge sending us back to do a right thing if it sent the other people back to do a wrong thing? This is making my head hurt, Bugg.'

'And mine,' says Dilan.

'Because, because . . .' I say, trawling my brains. 'Because it didn't know they were going to do a bad thing when it sent them. It probably thought they were going to do something innocent – like visit their granny, or plant a tree or something.'

Dilan rubs his head and sniffs the air, as if he could smell a crazy idea. 'You're completely mad, Bugg, but you may be right.'

'O–K,' says Lorna, doubt plastered across her face. 'So what do we do now?'

Chapter 26

Lorna's scream is very good. It sends prickles down my back.

'Look!' says the man behind me. 'Look, she's stuck – and the tide's coming in.'

'The poor little thing!' says his wife. 'Quick, call the coastguard, Ernest. There's a phone box up by the shops.' She turns and flaps her hands at the air. 'Help, help, there's a girl stuck on the footings of the pier! Help!'

Ernest runs for the phone box. More people gather to stare and shout at Lorna, who is doing a full-on impersonation of someone stuck, which indeed she might be by now. 'Help!' says Dilan feebly.

'Help,' I echo, watching the people, in case any of them are trying to set fire to the pier.

'The phone box is bust!' yells Ernest. 'Ruddy kids have broken the phone off.' He holds out a black telephone receiver with a tangle of red wires dangling beneath.

'Help!' calls Lorna. 'The sea's rising.' Water laps around the concrete post she's clinging to. It looks as if she might truly be in trouble.

'I'll run down to the one in Station Road,' says another man.

'Fat lot of good that'll do,' says a third. 'It was vandalised last night.'

'I could go to the doctor's surgery,' says a woman.

'You need the firemen,' says another. 'They've got ladders. Hang on there, girly, we'll have you off in a jiffy.'

'What about Dave?' I mutter to Dilan. 'His dad's a fireman – he must know how to get hold of them.'

'Right,' says Dilan. 'Give me the tickets. I'll run and get him.'

Dilan vanishes into the crowd and I stand back and, with my eyes popping from staring, study every inch of the pier. I can't see anyone, and I can't see any sign of fire. Glancing back over my shoulder I see the town clock. Six forty-five. Within half an hour it should be well and truly ablaze. Surely it couldn't happen that fast.

Dilan and Dave rush out of the pier entrance. Dave jumps on his Chopper, pulling an accidental wheelie all the way along the promenade. 'He'll bring them,' says Dilan. 'I just hope it isn't too soon. Anything happened?'

I shake my head. 'I can't see anything.'

'What's that?' says Dilan, pointing towards a small orange boat bobbing out at sea.

It's an inflatable dinghy. It's difficult to make out which way it's heading. There's definitely someone on-board, but from this distance they're just a grey blob. 'I can't make them out,' I say.

Dilan's practically hanging over the railings. 'Nor me – although I think there's only one person.'

I rush to the sea telescope on the other side of the pier. '10p, it says. Have we got 10p?' I pull the last coins out of my pocket, and there, among the pennies, is a shiny old 10p piece. It slips into the slot and the telescope starts to tick.

'There – left a bit,' says Dilan, swinging the telescope around so that I can see the little orange dinghy. I twiddle with the focus until I identify the person on-board rowing towards us.

'Eddie Henderson,' I say.

'Where?' says Dilan.

'In the boat.'

'Let's see.' Dilan grabs the telescope and pushes me away. 'Blimey – he's really young.'

'Yes – but old enough to know what he's doing.'

'What?' asks Dilan.

'He's time-travelling, he shouldn't be here. When they investigate the fire, they'll find out that he's in bed asleep.'

'How do you know?' asks Dilan, still staring through the telescope.

'I went – oh – it's too complicated to explain now. What's he doing?'

'Getting closer.'

'And?' I say, peering at the figure in the boat.

'He's got something in his hands. It might be a petrol can . . . I'm not sure.'

I imagine the speed of petrol flames. I've seen it plenty of times in the movies. It only takes a second for everything to go up.

'What do we do?' asks Dilan.

'We grab him. Red-handed.'

Chapter 27

It doesn't take long to find our way to the door at the back of the pier. Peering over the side, we can see Lorna's still clinging to her rock, although from here I can also see that she could easily wade to shore. 'Help,' she wails mournfully. If Miss Swanson from drama club saw this she'd give Lorna the lead in the Christmas show. It's a brilliant performance.

The little orange boat is bobbing a few feet from the first of the iron girders that hold the pier up out of the sea, but out of sight of all the people on the shore. From above, Eddie Henderson's intentions are quite clear. Two petrol cans, a load of sheets and some newspapers lie in the bottom of the dinghy. Enough to set practically anything on fire.

Lying on my stomach and peering between the floorboards, I watch Henderson drift under the iron girders until his boat reaches the older wooden posts that are right beneath the pier and reach up into the structure.

Dilan flattens himself against the deck and stares through the gaps. 'He's tying the boat up,' he says.

I look back towards the shore. The fire engine's there; Lorna's in the arms of an enormous man dressed from head to toe in yellow and the crowd is cheering.

But the man in the boat's not interested. He's ripping the sheets into long strips and tying them around the legs of the pier, right below the ballroom.

'Why can't they see what he's doing?' asks Dilan.

'The ballroom's so large that no one can see what happens underneath the pier, just like they can't see us. He can do what he likes. No one'll know until they see the smoke,' I say, looking around for anything that would help us. There's a lifebelt, and a stack of rotting wood, and strapped to a post is something that might be an emergency flare.

'Any idea how these things work?' I ask.

Dilan grabs it off me and bashes the end against the wooden deck. A shower of sparks springs from the end, belching smoke and stink, and then three little pompoms of orange fire leap high into the evening sky.

I watch them and then look back towards the shore. People are pointing at us.

'Here,' I shout, jumping into the air and pointing down at my feet. 'HE'S TRYING TO SET FIRE TO THE PIER!'

Dilan leaps up and down and waves his arms. 'BELOW US – in a boat!'

I don't suppose for one minute that they can hear us, but two firemen break into a slow run along the promenade and stop up by the telescope.

I wave again, and look down towards the boat below.

He's pouring the petrol onto the sheets he wrapped around the pier, and plenty more of it is falling onto the sea, spreading in a great lethal rainbow across the waves.

'He's got petrol!' I shout.

'Yes,' says Dilan. 'Petrol!'

Over by the promenade railings, I can see Dave Dando pulling at one of the firemen and pointing. Together they run for the little collection of upside-down rowing boats clustered on the beach.

'Yes!' I shout, just as Eddie Henderson rows away from the pier, hidden by the decking until he reaches the very end and the open sea.

And, just as he throws the match . . .

Chapter 28

Dave Dando's dad was a rowing champion when he was younger, which is just as well, because he and Dave and a fire extinguisher reach us at the same time as the first flames lick up over the boards of the pier.

Seconds later we're in the boat and a huge jet of water arrives from the fire engine, which has moved along the promenade and is now drenching the pier.

'Who was it?' says Dave's dad.

'Eddie Henderson? I think,' I say.

Dave's dad picks the radio out of his yellow coat and says things like 'Henderson boy', 'roger' and 'tango' and 'south-easterly direction'.

Dave looks adoringly at his dad, who pats Dave on the head. 'Good work, son,' he says, turning the boat for the shore.

I look back at the fire. Smoke curls into the sky, but in a slow, tired way. Beyond the pier, I can see Eddie Henderson rowing like crazy, but another boat is catching him up, this time with an outboard motor, three men in yellow and a man in a uniform.

'Good work,' says Dave's dad. 'Good work.'

The sand bumps the bottom of the boat and we jump out into the arms of feather-clad women and black-suited men.

'Bravo!'

'Sensational!'

'Magnificent!'

Dragged from the rowing boat, we stumble up to the entrance of the pier, bowled along by the feathers and perfume until we're rammed into the ballroom and seated in the front row.

'Would you like some lemonade?' asks a woman. 'Some toffee?'

'What about a Walnut Whip?' asks another.

Lorna wriggles in next to us, slightly damp, but grinning from ear to ear.

I grin back.

A giant voice booms through the loudspeakers, '*Welcome, everyone! Starting a little late, but not to worry. Here in the Castle Ballroom, Shabbiton, I'd like to present our first couple in the Frank Darnell Competition cup, competing for the tango – Verity Cowley and* Derek *Simmons!*'

The house lights dim and a giant spotlight centres in on the dance floor. From somewhere in the darkness a real orchestra strikes up, and a woman in a magenta backless dress trots onto the floor, her hand held by a tall, suited man with an enormous moustache. They whisk, whirl, tremble, and the audience gasps in appreciation. The woman bends backwards until her tightly pulled bun brushes the floor, her partner tosses her over his head as if she weighed as little as the sequins on her tights.

When they finish the audience erupts into an ecstasy of clapping.

'Quite good,' says Dave, chomping a toffee. 'For dancing.'

'*And now, the Castle Ballroom's very own Arnold Wells – and Doreen Golightly. Take your places, please.*'

They sizzle. There's no other word I can use to describe what's happening in front of my eyes. Granddad and Miss Golightly, the school secretary, sizzle. Every movement is crisp and dynamic. I know, from watching Granddad's videos, that their shoulder lines are perfect, that her leg lifts are spot on, that their faces are showing exactly the right level of superiority and that their eyes are meeting and burning with passion.

For the whole time that they dance, I don't breathe. I don't think anyone here does. This is perfection. What we're seeing is a dance that'll be remembered forever. One that wouldn't have taken place if the fridge hadn't sent us back.

When they finish, she's almost flat on the ground, their fingertips touching. There's a silence before the audience cascades into roaring applause. They stand, they clap, they shout, they slap each other on the back, while Granddad and Miss Golightly bow slightly to the judges and disappear into the darkness.

'Gordon Bennett,' says Dave.

'Exactly,' says Dilan, wiping what I know is a tear from his eye.

'Was that your Granddad?' whispers Lorna. But I can't answer, because I've got a huge lump in my throat.

Chapter 29

We leave before the end. It's Dilan's idea. He says, quite rightly, that we can't afford to get caught up in what happens next. We need to get away before we mess up time. I feel sad as we turn our backs on the pier. Watching Granddad dance was like. . . well, like a rainbow, or Christmas, or eating baked potatoes round a bonfire.

'I'd like to have found out who won, what happened,' says Lorna.

'But you will,' says Dilan. 'In the present – Granddad'll tell us. At least he'll have something to say when we get back, and we might actually understand some of it.'

'What are you blathering on about?' says Dave.

Dilan blushes red and clamps his hand over his mouth. 'Nothing,' he says.

Dave looks at us doubtfully.

I say nothing. Anything I say is bound to make things worse. We've committed a major time-sin. We've made friends with someone from the past and hinted that we're from the future. I'm sure that's not allowed.

Dave pinches his brow. 'Something odd about you lot.'

'Is there?' says Lorna.

'Hmm, can't put my finger on it. Those shorts for a start,' he says, pointing at Dilan's pants sticking out over the top.

We stand quietly. Personally I'm trying to think of a really good excuse for what Dilan just said.

'Anyway,' says Dave, 'got to get home for my tea. See you around.'

He pedals off and Dilan sighs with relief. 'Sorry,' he says.

'Anyway, we did it,' I say. 'We followed the instructions from the fridge. We made Arnold dance.'

'So do you think that's what it's all been about? Just getting Granddad to dance?' says Dilan, hoisting up his waistband.

I shrug. 'It does seem a lot of fuss for just one dance.'

We walk through a cold stretch of sea mist back home. The piles of bricks for building the estate loom up at us, and we have to follow the path carefully to find the house. We walk in almost silence, the distant music from the pier the only sound. Every now and then it stops and I pause to listen for the applause, turning around to see the faint yellow lights of the pier glowing through the mist.

I'd really like to be back there.

The house smells of dishcloths and boiling meat, and a suffocating warm steam catches my throat as we walk in. There are three yoghurts waiting for us in the fridge. They're modern ones and luckily, although the telly booms through the door from the lounge, no one appears.

'Ready?' I ask.

The other two nod and we dig into the pots of creamy,

rich yoghurt.

I keep my eyes on the floor. It changes from blue and white squares to modern brown tiles, and as it changes I'm aware of a new silence – one that shouldn't be here in the twenty-first century. No telly. No booming dance music. 'Granddad?' I say, opening the door to the lounge.

But it's Mum sitting on the couch. Reading a book, her feet up on the end, looking happy and relaxed.

'Mum?'

'Yes, darling?'

'Nothing,' I say, retreating back into the kitchen and staring at Dilan and Lorna. 'Granddad's not on the sofa,' I say.

'Does that mean we've done something to him?' says Dilan. 'Surely we haven't . . .'

'Oh dear. Have we lost him somewhere? Is he in time limbo?' says Lorna, her eyes wide with worry.

For a moment I contemplate the possibility. 'I don't see how we could have done.'

'Perhaps he ate a yoghurt?' she says. 'You never know.'

'Perhaps he's in his room?' says Dilan, pushing past me into the lounge. 'Hi, Mum,' he says, stomping over to the far side and opening Granddad's bedroom door. But it isn't Granddad's bedroom: it's a study. All neat and tidy and filled with wires and computers, not an old tissue in sight.

Perhaps Lorna's right, perhaps we have lost him. I feel deeply sad. Granddad was a wreck, an old shuffling man with dribble and stained cardigans, but I could still see glimpses of the young man and I wanted to tell him that, to tell him that I understood.

But he's gone.

I turn back towards the fridge. The letters are all mixed up. No words at all any more. Opening the door, I search for any more yoghurts, but all the food is ordinary, almost the same food that Dilan and I put in there, plus two bottles of champagne that we didn't.

Everything's almost the same, but slightly different. Like it is when you've been ill for a week and you wake up and come downstairs and someone's painted the kitchen a different colour.

'Do you think,' I whisper, 'that we've ended up in the future?'

'Is that possible?' asks Lorna.

I look out of the kitchen window, towards the sea. The estate's there, the apple tree's there – and so's the pier. White and shining in the evening sunlight. I look at the clock. Six fifteen. But when?

A car crunches onto the gravel outside and we rush to the kitchen window. It's a sports car. A low, silver thing with a soft roof and huge tyres. The driver's door opens and a tall man in a smart grey mac springs out and opens the passenger door. I can't see his face, but I can see the legs of the passenger. Long elegant legs with slim ankles belonging to a fine woman in her sixties. She's Miss Golightly without the years of peanut brittle. She's wearing a camel-coloured coat and perfectly applied lipstick. She looks a million dollars. The man turns towards us and holds out his elbow.

It's Granddad.

He's still an old man, but he's not. He's not bent and dribbling and sad. He's upright, and sprightly, and has a playful smile. Together they walk towards the front door.

Chapter 30

'Granddad,' I say, opening the door. 'How are you?'

'Grand, Sky, never been grander.' He leans forward and pats me on the head. 'Get out the sparkly glasses, Oliver, and we can have a toast – it's our anniversary.'

Dilan and I stare at each other.

'Oliver?' I say.

'Your brother, Sky,' says Miss Golightly, skipping past into the lounge. 'Get your brother to do it. Hello, Lorna, dear, are you going to join us?'

'Doreen, Arnold,' says Mum, springing up from the sofa, which is when I realise she's pregnant.

'Stay there, pet,' says Miss Golightly. 'Sky'll sort some snacks, won't you, dear?' she looks at me, so I turn and walk mechanically into the kitchen. Sky? My name is Sky? I like that – it's about a million times better than Bugg.

I open the noodle cupboard, and instead of packets of instant noodles there are crisps and cheese straws. I open a bag and empty them into a bowl.

Sky.

Sky.

Sky Wells.

It really is a whole lot better than Bugg Wells.

And then Dad appears holding a bottle of champagne, and we all get some, and we clink glasses, and Dad says, 'Forty years! Here's to Dad and lovely Doreen and forty fantastic years.' And Granddad gives Doreen a peck on the cheek, and she kisses him back properly on the mouth and I have to sit down.

'Speech!' says Mum.

'Speech!' says Dad, hugging Doreen as if she was his real mum.

'Oh yes, Arnold, dear, do give us a few words,' says Miss Golightly.

Granddad clears his throat, takes a sip of his champagne and points at a faded colour photograph on the wall, which I have never seen before.

'2nd July 1974.' He lifts the photo from the wall and holds it in his hand as if it could transfer the memory to his fingertips. 'What an evening! What a competition!'

'Go on then, love,' says Miss Golightly. 'Tell them. Tell them all about it.'

'It was a clear evening. A capacity crowd. The hairspray was thick . . .'

'And the make-up,' says Miss Golightly with a giggle.

'Ted Mildenhall was there judging, and that woman Anita Smears, and the ballroom looked magnificent.'

'Oh, it did.' Miss Golightly smiles, remembering, so that the make-up in the corner of her eyes cracks.

Granddad gazes at Miss Golightly. 'And so did you,

Doreen.'

'And you, Arnold.'

'And then they stopped us,' says Granddad. 'Because of the fire.'

I nearly choke on a cheese straw. 'The fire?'

'That idiot Eddie Henderson, the one that works on the petrol pumps out at Asco, he was just a boy, thought he'd do for the pier so that the family garage could open up on the seafront. He'd vandalised the phone boxes too, done a proper job of it. Regular delinquent. It all came out in court, loads of witnesses, old John Dando saw him rowing away, but they'd never have caught him if it wasn't for the kids.'

'Kids?' says Lorna.

'Oh yes,' says Miss Golightly. 'There were two children on the pier. They let off a flare, so the firemen knew something was going on, and the firemen were only there because of a girl stuck on the rocks when the tide came in. All terribly lucky.'

Lorna goes bright red and splutters over a crisp.

'Imagine what would have happened otherwise,' says Dad, topping up the champagne glasses. 'It would have been an awful accident – all those people in the ballroom, and the whole thing made of wood.'

The adults stare into the middle distance as if imagining the town without a pier.

'Anyway, no one ever knew who those children were – they were never seen again,' says Granddad, with another mouthful of champagne.

'Really?' asks Dilan/Oliver. 'They had no idea?'

Granddad shakes his head. 'No – and the only person that might have known was Dave Dando, and he left town as soon as he could to go into fashion. Police talked to him of course, but he made no sense. His brother runs that surf shop in town. They've made a fortune from shorts, I believe.'

Dilan/Oliver turns and shows me the label on the side of his shorts. *Dando*. I nearly drop my thimbleful of champagne.

'Anyway, if it wasn't for those kids, we'd never have won, because when they let us all back into the building, Verity and Derek were off like they'd been wound up. They danced beautifully, I could barely fault them. Maybe his second lift was a trifle wobbly, but I think I'm picking holes.'

'No, they did,' agrees Miss Golightly. 'They danced like a dream. I remember thinking we couldn't possibly outdo them. But . . .'

'Then it was our turn, and I remember feeling the heat of the lights . . .'

'And the slight smell of petrol,' says Miss Golightly.

'Yes, that too. Maybe because we'd had to stop and start, we really went for it. We danced . . . we danced our socks off – I wish you kids could have seen us.' Miss Golightly nods her head in agreement. 'Verity and Derek's tango was a nine out of ten, but ours . . .' Granddad grasps a cheese straw and waves it, like a conductor. 'My heart was in my mouth when we set off – I tried not to look at Ted Mildenhall. I knew if I saw him I'd miss a beat, but we danced out of our skins, left them standing.'

'Perfect tens,' says Miss Golightly, sipping from her glass. 'Never happened before.'

'Our foxtrot was a nine,' says Granddad.

'And the paso doble,' says Miss Golightly.

'We swept the floor with the cha-cha – won the prize, won the money, won the whole series.' Granddad coughs and looks away.

'It was wonderful,' says Miss Golightly, springing to her feet and hugging Granddad's elbow.

'It was the beginning of the TV career of course,' says Granddad. 'We never looked back after that, did we, dear?'

'No,' says Miss Golightly. 'And forty years of married life later, you can still take my breath away.'

Granddad married to the school secretary. I have to sit down again.

I think back to the last few hours, or days depending on which way you look at it. So much has changed. Everything's changed. I look at Mum's great pregnant bump. That wasn't part of the plan. I wasn't expecting a new baby in the family. I suppose it'll mean I'm not the youngest any more, which will be quite nice. There should be someone more scared than me, someone to keep me company behind the sofa. And Granddad's not living with us – he's living with Miss Golightly, except I suppose she's Mrs Wells.

I still can't get used to how young they look.

Mum goes over to the stereo and puts on a CD. It's a waltz.

Miss Golightly puts down her handbag and puts one hand on Granddad's shoulder and another on his arm. Granddad puts his free arm around her waist and together they dance the most perfect circle around the coffee table.

Dad holds Mum's arm and they blunder into an

uncomfortable shuffling.

Lorna stuffs another cheese straw in her mouth.

I realise I haven't worried about anything for at least an hour and go out to check on the fridge.

It's not humming. It's utterly silent.

I open the door. The light stays off. And there are no yoghurt pots, only ordinary recent shopping.

A trickle of water slips from underneath the vegetable compartment at the bottom and pools on the floor.

I press the button for the light, but no matter how hard I try, I can't make it come on.

'C'mon, fridge,' I say. 'Wake up.'

Still no hum.

I slam the door shut. In case it brings the fridge to life, but nothing happens except that some of the plastic letters from the door fall to the floor.

SHNAKT.

KNASHT.

I place them back onto the door, and the fridge lets out a long shuddering sigh.

THANKS

Fleur Hitchcock

Born in Chobham, by an airfield, and raised in Winchester on the banks of the River Itchen, Fleur Hitchcock grew up as the youngest child of three. When she was eight, she wrote a story about an alien and a jelly. It was called THE ALIEN AND THE JELLY and filled four exercise books. She grew up a little, went away to school near Farnham, studied English in Wales, and, for the next twenty years, sold Applied Art in the city of Bath. When her younger child was seven, she embarked on the Writing for Young People MA at Bath Spa and graduated with a distinction. Now living outside Bath, between parenting and writing, Fleur works with her husband, a toy-maker, looks after other people's gardens and grows vegetables.

Fleur's debut novel SHRUNK! was *The Sunday Times* 'Book of the Week', and you can follow her at: http://www.fleurhitchcock.wordpress.com or on Twitter: @fleurhitchcock